THE LEGEND OF LEJUBE ROGUE

The winter nights were dark and long, and when the fires had dwindled to ash and ember, the pioneers huddled close. They whispered fearsome tales of Lejube Rogue, the white Indian who ghosted through the untamed land seeking the man who had murdered his father and ravaged his mother, the man he had sworn to kill. Calling him demon or hero, the settlers told of the ice-eyed gunfighter and his incredible deeds — and perhaps some of the strange tales were even true.

PATRICIA LUCAS WHITE

◆

THE LEGEND OF LEJUBE ROGUE

Complete and Unabridged

LINFORD
Leicester

First published in the
United States of America in 2000

First Linford Edition
published 2002

British Library CIP Data

White, Patricia Lucas
    The legend of Lejube Rogue.—
    Large print ed.—
    Linford western library
    1. Western stories
    2. Large type books
    I. Title
    813.5'4 [F]

    ISBN 0–7089–9855–0

Published by
F. A. Thorpe (Publishing)
Anstey, Leicestershire

Set by Words & Graphics Ltd.
Anstey, Leicestershire
Printed and bound in Great Britain by
T. J. International Ltd., Padstow, Cornwall

This book is printed on acid-free paper

Oregon, 1873

The winter winds cried and mourned. The cold, inscrutable mountains kept their own secrets. The nights were dark and long, and when the fires had dwindled to ash and ember, the pioneers huddled close. They whispered fearsome tales of Lejube Rogue, the white Indian who ghosted through the untamed land seeking the man who had murdered his father and seduced his mother. The man Rogue had sworn to kill.

Calling him demon or hero, speaking from fear or admiration, the settlers told many strange tales of the ice-eyed gunfighter and his incredible deeds — and perhaps some of the tellings were even true.

Or perhaps the truth was stranger still.

1

Shifting the Spencer carbine to the crook of his left arm, Rogue nudged Ghost with his heels. He urged the dapple-gray stallion on up the narrow track, a deer trail meandering through the high Cascades, leading them in the general direction of their unknown quarry. The August sun was high, pooling shadows at the feet of the towering firs and pines, and already too warm for actual comfort. Despite the sweat that beaded on his forehead and the deer flies that weren't shy about feasting on his exposed flesh, minor discomforts didn't hold a patch to the rest of Rogue's worries.

The forest distorted sound, muffled it, hid its origin, but Rogue wasn't completely deceived — he couldn't afford to be, not when his life depended on it. He rode on, slow and cautious, eyes narrow, seeing everything and appreciating nothing of the brooding forest's beauty. He would save that for later, when he found out who had been doing the shooting he had heard a little more than an hour before and knew the why of it.

Likely it had been hunters, but he had to be sure. Where he was — high up in the volcanic mountains, old pumice spewed out hundred of years before deadening the thump of Ghost's hooves — was a long way from where folks usually hung out, but he had to be sure. A man like him didn't keep on living by taking foolish chances.

The breeze, scarcely strong enough to flutter aspen leaves, carried a new sound, one that sent little shivers to dance on Rogue's backbone. He didn't know what it was, but he did know it wasn't right. Leaning forward, he tried to peer through the curtain of green that hid what lay ahead, but could see very little. He sniffed the air. Dust and pine. Nothing out of the ordinary.

The slither and drag of sound came again, came from every direction and none, but it was close. Too close to ease Rogue's mind or to keep the prickles away from the back of his neck. Prickles that told him danger was near.

Whuffling softly, tossing his head, Ghost took a single step forward before he stopped, nostrils flaring, ears back, and stared straight ahead. It was all the warning Rogue needed.

Sliding off the stallion's blanketed back, Rogue was on the ground and moving between one heartbeat and the next, crouched low and moving toward the danger, not away.

Less than six feet ahead of where Ghost stood, the deer path intersected a slightly broader, better-used track. It was scuffed and torn, with deep furrows gouged in its whitish-gray surface. Blood, wet and red, glistened on the huckleberry brush beside the trail, darkened in the hoof marks that scarred its floor. From somewhere off to Rogue's right came a rasping, choking sound. An ugly, hurty sound that shouldn't rightly belong to a human being — but probably did. Either that or to a gut-shot critter dragging itself off to die.

The sweat that trickled down the sides of his face and under the neck of his buckskin shirt was pure ice; so was the knot in his stomach. Feeling real sick, like something bad was about to happen, Rogue stepped out onto the broader trail. His moccasins cushioning his soundless steps, he followed the blood spoor to its source.

A faint breeze whispered in the tops of the massive trees. A scrub jay scolded raucously. A gray pine-cutter chittered and scrambled up the trunk of a yellow pine. But Rogue's full attention was focused on the source of another sound — one that spoke of pain and dying.

An odd sense of foreboding touched him even before Rogue saw the boy belly-crawling along the trail, leaving life's blood to mark his passage. The sense had no real name, but Rogue recognized it, knew it was what the man of power, Eagle Flying, his teacher and friend, had once seen in a long-ago vision, foretold as truth. Rogue's feet had already set him on the path to his own doom, and there was no turning back.

A muscle jumping in his jaw, his pale eyes bleak, Rogue accepted the inevitable. He approached the boy, but only after he had swept the surroundings with a critical eye, examined every bush and tree for a lurking enemy. *And did it all with the carbine at ready.*

The boy was alone. His hands, broken-nailed and bleeding, reached out, clawed at the earth. His young muscles corded as he dragged himself forward an inch or two at a time. One leg pushed, but the other, blood-soaked, trailed uselessly, the toe of his boot furrowing the ground as he moved relentlessly onward.

'Kid?' Rogue called softly. There was no answer. The boy just stretched out his arms, dug his fingers into the gritty soil, and pulled himself toward some unknown destination.

Leaning down, Rogue touched the kid's shoulder, felt the warmth of his blue shirt, the pain of the young body underneath, and said again, a little louder, but not loud enough to carry beyond their immediate vicinity, 'Kid!'

A young face, its features masked in blood and dirt, turned toward Rogue, and pale-blue eyes, pain-glazed and near madness, stared up at him. 'Let me go,' a cracked, still-high voice choked out. 'I'll kill them. Kill them all.' The head, topped with rough black hair, dropped down, and the boy reached out and began his slow, dragging movement again. And again fresh blood dripped from his wounded leg.

Distancing himself from the fury that was beginning to burn within him, white-hot fury at the devils who had shot the boy and left him to die alone, Rogue reached down with his left hand. He took the boy by the shoulder, halted his progress. 'Kid,' he said, working at keeping his voice soft and gentle, 'I don't know where you're heading in such an all-fired hurry, but you're hurt bad. You've got to stop long enough for me to do something about that leg.'

'No. Can't stop. They took-took . . . ' His voice shrilled into silence. His hands convulsed and pawed at the ground, but he had reached the end of his strength. He gasped in a breath, his knotted muscles relaxed completely, and he slumped, lay quiet and still, face down in the dirt.

Turning the limp body to its back, Rogue knelt on one knee and felt for the weakly throbbing pulse in the boy's tanned neck. The kid was still alive, if barely, but Rogue couldn't do any real doctoring in the middle of the trail — especially when the prickles in back of his neck were growing steadily stronger. Transferring the carbine to his left hand, Rogue picked up the boy as if he weighed no more than the gun and headed back the way he had come.

Rogue whistled a single, low-pitched note to summon Ghost and the loaded pack horse that waited with him, and they followed him as he shouldered his way into a dense thicket of young fir. They pushed through the thick, yielding growth until they reached a sun-filled clearing near the middle of the stand of man-high trees.

It looked like a good place to stay out of sight and do what needed doing. Partially carpeted in dry grass, it had a spring with water for drinking and washing, and something else Rogue hadn't expected but was real glad to see: the run-off from the spring bubbled into a sandy basin beside a large windfall and had cut its way into the earth. Heavy winter rains and melting snows had widened and deepened the channel, forming a shallow cave beneath the log.

The boy moaned once when Rogue eased him down onto the matted grass. Working swiftly, not really sure how much time the kid had left, he leaned the Spencer against the log, jerked his bedroll off the pack animal, and spread it on the sandy floor of the cave. He carried the boy to the rough bed and slashed open the leg of his dirty, blood-stained pants.

The kid had been shot, right enough. The bullet had torn through the thigh, ripping flesh and muscle, but as far as Rogue could tell, it hadn't touched the bone. Deep within the wound, a tiny blood vessel spurted red with every beat of the boy's heart. Even as Rogue probed the wound and cleaned bits of dirt from the injury, the blood flow weakened, slowed to the barest trickle.

Rogue felt bleakness creep up from his heart, stare out his eyes, and harshen the planes of his face. He frowned, then took a deep breath and let it out slow. The lead had slashed a long, jagged path, severed veins, and just about bled the kid dry. Very soon it would do what it was meant to do and kill him.

Shaman and healer Eagle Flying had

11

found Rogue dying in the desert, had healed his wounds, and had taught him much — but not enough, not nearly enough. They had been forced to part too soon, to part before young Patrick Scanlon (the boy Rogue had been) had the time to learn but a few of the ways of power. *Or to master the power Eagle Flying had swore he bore within himself: the power to heal, and more.*

Healing wasn't an easy thing to do, and he was ill-prepared, but he had to try. The kid wasn't more than eleven or twelve, skinny as a post, and too damned young to die. Rogue's own killing business would just have to wait.

'I can't let him die,' Rogue said, speaking the words aloud, not even pretending he was talking to the grazing horses. The packhorse ignored him, but Ghost raised his head, pricked his ears forward, and watched the man for a second or two before he began tearing at the grass again.

Tired beyond all knowing, tired of being alone, of searching for the man he had vowed to kill, tired of everything his life had become, Rogue fought back a sigh and began his preparations. After he had mounded dried grass and twigs into a loose pile, Rogue kindled a small fire on the sand very near where the unconscious boy lay. Taking a leather pouch and some clean cloths from the pack, Rogue stood without moving for a small space of time. He tried to figure if what he was doing was the best way — even though he already knew it was the only way. At least, it was the only way he knew.

Only then did he allow some of the old teaching to seep back into his brain, remind him of what he had lost. Crouching between the boy and the fire, he muttered, 'I could have done this once. Eagle Flying taught me well, but so much has . . . Mayhap the power is gone like . . . ' His words of doubt fell away as he began to concentrate, to remember each step of the road toward healing.

Reaching into the beaded pouch, he

pulled out a handful of pungent herbs. Some he threw into the tiny fire, letting the smoke curl up around him; the rest he crushed in his clenched fist. Mouthing old medicine words, invoking powers and spirits beyond sight and knowing, he spread the brownish powder on a pad of wet cloth. Applying the resulting poultice to the boy's wound, he held it in place with a steady, even pressure.

As he breathed in the aromatic smoke, Rogue's eyes closed, and an old chant for healing rose in his throat. He chanted, without pause, for a very long time. The sing-song words were low and monotonous and seemed almost soundless in the heated summer still-ness. Dizzy and light-headed from the smoke, Rogue chanted until he felt the power build, mystical power that filled him, flowed through his body. When it was at its peak, some of Rogue's strength left him, poured through his hand into the boy.

After a time, the kid moved weakly,

opened his eyes, and stared up blankly. 'What happened?' he mumbled thickly.

Rogue stopped chanting but kept his big hand pressed against the blood-stained cloth. 'Somebody shot you,' Rogue answered, 'but I reckon you'll make it now.' Although there wasn't a trace of feeling in his hoarse voice, Rogue felt nothing but pleasure. His power was still there, hidden away beneath the white man's teachings, and he was glad. Maybe when his hunt was over, when his father's killer was dead, he could go back to the desert and find Eagle Flying. Maybe it wasn't too late after all.

The boy's next question brought Rogue back to the moment, 'Who are you? Are you an Indian?'

Was he an Indian? Releasing his hold on the poultice, Rogue shook his head and started to stand, but the healing, done without the rites of purification, had taken too much of his strength. Rogue sank back down and sat on the sand beside the boy's makeshift bed.

'Don't move. The bleeding has stopped, but . . . I'll change the bandage soon, but for now, it'd be best if you don't tear around any.'

The boy nodded, lay still for a long moment, and then returning memory jabbed at him. He got his elbows down and tried to push himself up. 'I said, don't move,' Rogue growled, pushing the kid back onto the pallet.

'No!' The kid's yell would have put a screech owl to shame. 'You can't keep me here. I have to get up and . . . '

'Stay there. After a bit, I'll go find your family and let them know . . . '

'Mister, you just don't understand. Those men, I don't know who they are, but there was a bunch of them, and they took my sister, Faith. I have to go find her, I promised I'd take care of her. I promised!' He struggled against the hand that held him, struggled a lot harder than Rogue would have thought possible.

'Damn it, boy, show some sense. Look at that leg of yours — just how far

16

do you think you could get on that?'

The boy was silent for a moment or two, and then a fresh torrent of words poured out of his mouth. 'Then you go after her. Leave me here and . . . Please, don't let them hurt her. She's just a little girl and . . . ' The boy's voice fell to an agonized whisper, and his dirty hands went up to cover his face, to wipe furtively at the tears that were trying to spill out of his eyes.

The sun was bright and hot. The sky was blue, untarnished by clouds. The wind was murmuring in the treetops. But Rogue still felt the shadow of impending doom, knew, with the trace of power that was still upon him, that he had already taken too many steps down that path of destiny. Sadness touched him. He had searched for so long, it was hard to put his own vows aside and take up a new banner, especially now when he knew he was close. It had to be done, didn't it? The boy's need was greater than his own, wasn't it?

And the boy's next words took away all of Rogue's doubts. 'One of those men is crazy, mister. He laughed when he shot me, and he laughed even harder when he grabbed Faith by the hair and sort of swung her around before he took her away.' The boy shuddered at his memories and then he said, his voice real quiet, 'Poor little kid. She fought like a wildcat, but she only screamed once. Mister, please, do something.'

He was going to do just what the kid had asked, but he needed to know one more thing. Rogue leaned forward, looked deep into the eyes that were almost mirror images of his own. 'Do you know who I am?'

'No, and I don't care. I'd ask Lejube Rogue or the devil himself for help right now and . . . ' Suddenly realizing what he had said, the boy dropped his hand to Rogue's arm and flushed painfully. 'I didn't mean that you were evil-like . . . ' he stammered. 'I'm sorry, mister. I just . . . ' He tried to get up.

Rogue just held the struggling boy in place, refused to allow him to re-injure himself. Finally the kid gave up the fight and lay there, gulping back tears, trying hard not to sob openly. 'My mama is real sick,' he said. 'She's been sick for a long time. If those men hurt her little girl, Mama will die. She's already lost . . . Please, mister.'

'Hush, now, and try to get some sleep. I've got a few things to do so you'll be safe here. When I'm done, I'll go see what's happened to your little sister. I'll save her if I can.'

Trying to smile through his tears, the boy looked Rogue straight in the face and said, with nothing but pure trust and absolute faith in his voice, 'Thanks, mister. I know you can.'

2

Rogue looked back once. There wasn't a single hoofprint or bent twig left to lead any searchers to the fir thicket. The boy would be safe. He had jerky and baked camas root to eat, the bedroll to ward off the chill of the mountain nights, water for drinking, the pack horse to keep him company, and the Spencer carbine and a few extra cartridges for protection.

Guiding Ghost through the open timber, paralleling the trail left by the kidnappers, Rogue felt a momentary dizziness. The healing had left him weak. He knew he should be resting, but time was too important to allow that now. He had to find where they had taken the little girl and rescue her if it was at all possible. If it killed him. He couldn't fail the trust he had seen in the boy's eyes, neither could he break this new promise. He had made it while the power was still upon him, and Eagle Flying had made sure Patrick Scanlon understood exactly what that meant. The old shaman had told him more than once: promises made under the power, no matter how grave or how trivial, bound the promiser for an eternity.

★ ★ ★

Rogue studied the tracks left by the retreating outlaws for what had to be the tenth time, read sign that should have made sense but damned sure didn't. Staring at the hoof-torn, well-marked trail, he tried to puzzle it out and then, pondering it still, shook his head and rode on.

Oregon was a new land, and rich. It attracted its full share of drifters, outlaws, and hardcases, as well as more honest men, but still and all, most of them wouldn't willingly harm a child. And yet, the dozen or so men who had left a plainly-marked trail for him to follow had done exactly that: they, or at least one of them, had shot an unarmed boy and left him to die a slow and painful death all by his lonesome.

To make it worse, they had stolen a little girl. That act alone branded them outcasts and raised every decent man's hand against them. The gang of owlhoots had to know that, but if they knew, why hadn't they tried to conceal their tracks? Unless the whole thing was nothing more than a trap.

Rogue allowed himself a thin smile. The trap had been set all right, but it hadn't been set for him. It hadn't been set for *Lejube Rogue, the demon who walked the mountains*.

His smile tightened for a fraction of a second. He knew what else folks said about him, calling him, among other things, the demon who had no fear, no soul, and no love to stay his hand. The white Indian who killed without mercy or compassion. 'Maybe so,' he muttered. 'Maybe this time they've got it right.'

A glowing ball of blinding orange, the sun had slid an hour closer to the western mountains and looked like it was getting ready to plunge behind them real soon. Rogue pulled the stallion to a halt and took in a breath of air, testing it for some new sign. Dust and something more tickled the inside of his nose. His smile was grim with satisfaction when he reckoned it as the faintest hint of acrid wood smoke, campfire smoke with the scent of cooking lodged in its middle.

He was getting close and intended to get closer — and did, with every step Ghost took. When the smoky odor was an almost visible veil drifting among the towering trees, Rogue turned the gray to the right and rode deeper into the virgin timber, away from the trail. As he hoped, the hillside grew progressively steeper, more overgrown with brush and vines, and made a good hiding place for the big horse when Rogue continued the search on foot.

Dismounting, Rogue led Ghost into a tiny stream and up its course until they reached a cleft in its undercut bank and climbed out into a small glade. There, Rogue untied the buckskin strap that held the hackamore in place, setting the horse free.

As he turned to walk away, what Eagle Flying had called 'the seeing power' struck, took him to his knees. The sunlight darkened, was replaced by something more, something forged of the power, something that forced Rogue to do what he should have done before. His doom shadowing his tomorrows, Lejube Rogue began to chant his death song.

The stallion snorted, nudged Rogue's shoulder, and tore him away from the medicine dream. The chant dying on his lips, he struggled to his feet and leaned against the great horse for a moment or two, fighting against the dizziness, the weakness that still held him. It passed.

'Wait for me as along as you are able,'

he said, speaking as if the animal understood every word. Sliding his hand down Ghost's sleek shoulder in a gesture of farewell, Rogue turned slowly, hung the hackamore on a dogwood tree, walked away, and left the horse staring after him.

Picking his way back down the gully, Rogue tried to remember more of Eagle Flying's teachings, but more pressing needs kept them away. The girl, Faith, came first. After she was found . . . he had no answer for that nor any time to worry it; besides, his death song had been sung and, as other men had said before him, *it was a good day to die.*

A mile or so later, moving almost as silently as the gray smoke that eddied and drifted up from the canyon below, Rogue slipped through the Douglas firs that blanketed the hillside. The trees were old and big, and the dry moss that hung from their lower limbs fluttered briefly in the wind of his passage, but nothing else betrayed him. The needle-slick forest floor was littered with the debris of forgotten storms, but long practice allowed him to work his way down the treacherous slope with the sure grace of a mountain lion.

As he moved from tree to tree, a bluejay shrieked a shrill territorial warning. Rogue froze. A gray squirrel chattered an angry reply. Rogue released his pent breath. He waited, unmoving, listening for man-sound, but there was none: creaking trees, droning deer flies, rustling leaves, and the eternal whine of mosquitoes. He moved on, and every step he took increased his certainty he was walking into a trap, a trap never set for him — a trap that might not be strong enough to hold him.

There would be time enough to test the truth of that, but for now his thoughts had to be focused on a more immediate danger. The canyon was close. Rogue touched the walnut handles of two Army Colts belted around his middle, seated them snugly within their oiled holsters, then spread his inches belly-down on the ground. Wiggling and squirming, he forced his way beneath the intertwined wild lilac and buck brush that capped a rocky promontory to catch a good look at what waited down in the canyon. Despite the care he exercised, pebbles rolled under his hands and dirt sifted down the granite cliff face when he parted the screen of brush at the canyon's brink.

If he had read the signs right, his search was coming to an end. Sounds, men shouting curses, an ax thudding into wood, the whinny of a horse, echoing, multiplied by the high canyon walls, all spoke of the presence of the outlaws — or at least, of men who had to be checked out before he could search further. The late afternoon shadows lay deep within the canyon, hiding everything except the greenish-blue reflection from a river that curled among house-size boulders and a billowing column of white smoke.

He would have to go down, examine

the canyon and its unseen occupants closer. Rogue had just started to wiggle his way back from the rim when the jay screeched again. Motionless, listening for the cause of the new alarm, he waited. It could be just another argument between bird and squirrel, but he couldn't afford to take any chances. He waited. Within seconds, the volcanic earth beneath his tense body vibrated with the sound of approaching horses — and there were no wild horses in this part of Oregon.

Lying full-length in the scant concealment of the brush, Rogue sweated, but not from fear. The weltering sun was hot. Moisture gathered beneath his leather shirt, oozed down his backbone, beaded and ran on his face, but he didn't try to wipe it away — not even when it stung his narrowed eyes.

Somewhere behind him bushes swished and raked against moving animals. The jay's scolding rose to a frenzy, but the riders kept right on talking. Rogue couldn't see them, hoped they wouldn't spot him, but he could hear every word that passed between the two men.

'Dammit, Slim, I told you I ain't got no liking for this. The whole damned country is gonna be hot on our tails, and I cain't say that I blame 'em. Stealing that little girl away from her family just ain't right, and we both know it,' one of the riders said.

The other one kept his voice low, making it a little hard for Rogue to hear. 'Naw, it ain't, but we're getting paid real good, so just keep on riding guard on this side of the canyon like we was told. We need that damned money, and it ain't like that kid is going to get hurt or nothing.'

'Gold or no gold, it ain't right. That poor little tike, just sitting there, all tied up, staring at nothing. Hell, man, she's scared half to death, and I don't blame her. I think the old man is crazy enough to do something real bad to her, and that fool nephew of his ain't a lick better. The way he goes sneaking around like a whipped dog plumb gives me the creeps.'

Slim's voice was a little louder and held a strong undertone of what could only be fear. 'Why don't you just shut your yap and light a shuck out of here, Kale? Likely if you ride fast enough and far enough, the old man can't gut-shoot you like the yellow-belly you are and leave you dying like he did that boy. But me, I ain't about to . . . '

The horses walked on and took the two men out of earshot, but Rogue didn't move at once. He waited until he was sure they were gone before he got untangled and moved out into the open. The guards had been riding east, what had to be up the canyon, so he turned west.

This part of the Cascade Mountains was new country as far as he was concerned. He had to scout the canyon, discover an easy way down its walls. He could climb down the cliffs — there were handholds, ledges, and fissures everywhere in the stone — but that was out. He had to plan ahead, plan a route that would prove safe for a scared little girl, a child with no real reason to trust him any more than she did her captors.

The shadows had grown a foot or so, and the sun was more than halfway down and sliding fast, but Rogue was still looking. He hadn't had a bit of luck. 'Just a little further, and I'll turn back, try to find something back the other way,' he told himself as he entered a grove of laurel.

Dry heaps of curling bark crackled and snapped beneath his feet. Just ahead, a buck started from his bed, snorted once, bounded over a fallen tree trunk, and disappeared.

Suddenly heartened, hope growing large in his mind, Rogue followed, found the narrow break in the canyon wall and the deer trail that wound and twisted its way between boulders and young trees, leading down. As he watched, the four-point, still running scared, emerged from the clumped willows that edged the river on the canyon floor.

Studying the switchbacks and the ravine below, Rogue figured it wasn't a path for old ladies. With twilight and a cloudless sky, he would have time and some to spare to finish the climb and find a place to hole up before full dark. He started down.

Before he had gone a dozen feet, he caught a blur of motion coming from up the canyon. Men. Mounted men. Coming down the canyon toward him. Riding slow and easy. Looking real peaceful, like they didn't have a care in the world. Rogue crouched down, took shelter behind a puny young tree and scarcely larger rock, and watched them until they rounded a bend far down the canyon and were out of sight.

Only then did he give a soundless whistle. The riders, hardcases every one, had been heavily armed with both rifles and Colts. They were leading extra horses, carrying a goodly amount of supplies of some sort. But there hadn't been a child in that bunch, and Rogue had looked hard and good. She was still somewhere in the canyon — and he doubted very much she was alone. 'What in blazes is going on?' he muttered.

There must have been thirty men in the bunch, more than enough to be a small army. It was a new senseless piece for the already senseless puzzle. Rogue didn't have time to do much more than worry it a little as he checked his own Colts before he slipped and slid his way down into the canyon. He knew damned well he was walking into a hair-triggered trap, one that would catch him square between two gangs of dangerous men if he wasn't real careful.

3

The shadows had deepened, but twilight still lingered as Rogue crawled and jumped his way across the rock-filled riverbed. Summer-low, the water was bone-chilling cold with snow melt from the surrounding mountain peaks, but it was sweet to the taste when he knelt and scooped up several handsful to quench his thirst.

The rocks that filled the channel loomed big and gray, and years of relentless action by the rushing waters of spring had eaten at them, leaving behind swirls, curves, and holes to mark their passage. Ages of flood had carved the huge stones into smooth, flowing shapes, wearing away all angles and softness until the rocks themselves had taken on the seeming of fluidity, had become one with the water.

Awe filled him. These were no petty,

rounded river rock to roll and tumble at the whim of every spate. These were gigantic monoliths, abstraction, sacred sculptures dedicated to primordial gods, earth gods.

Rogue stared at the gray monuments of stone, almost fell prey to a new bout of dizziness as the need rose within him, the terrible need to beg forgiveness for man's desecration of the holy place and to slink away. The place had the feel of old power, and Rogue was made small by the force and majesty of the great stones.

Bowing his head, Rogue took a deep, steadying breath, stood firm and let the power of the stones sink deep into his being, and then he silently thanked the stones. When the thanks was given, he was no longer an intruder. Rogue moved on up the canyon.

At that moment, Rogue and the canyon were one, and all the life that thrived there recognized him as a brother. An ouzel waded out from its underwater walk, stood on the graveled shore, teetering up and down, searching the clear water with beady eyes, hoping to sight another hellgrammite or some larva.

A large cutthroat trout, shining silver, hung in the swift water, barely moving for a long moment before it flipped its tail and darted for the concealing shadow of a rocky overhang.

Yellow flowers bloomed, massed and thick, on the grassy floodplain. And mountain blackberries, full ripe and glistening with sweet-tartness, hung heavy on sharp-briared vines, tempting him.

He was tempted, but Rogue had no time to stand and drink in the beauty and peace of the canyon or even to taste its bounty. He slipped through close-growing willows, edged around mossy stones. Cloaking his movement in every available shadow, he crept closer and closer to the soaring column of smoke that led him like a beacon.

Darkness rushed in and claimed the canyon just as Rogue climbed to the top of one of the massive boulders that ringed and protected the outlaw's camp. Their fire surged high, fed hungrily on pitchy pine logs, flung orange light in a great, flickering circle.

Shading his eyes against the sudden glare, Rogue raised his head, peered over the boulder, and assessed the camp. He looked for the kid and for danger. Seven men were there: five lounging on bedrolls, two perched high in the rocks, sitting like they were doing some guarding but not expecting much to happen. Firelight reflected from a large number of rifle barrels. A goodly share of the weapons were stacked on a tarp near the fire; others were held by the two men he had guessed were guards.

The camp had been there a while. With the amount of greasy bones, clothing, and garbage that already despoiled the site, it couldn't be new. A smoke-blackened coffeepot, crusted iron skillets, and a large iron kettle full of something sat on a rock close to the edge of the fire. It rested cheek to jowl with an untidy heap of dirty tin plates and cups and a few knives and spoons.

The shifting light glinted redly on whiskey bottles, some clutched in men's hands, some lying empty on the ground. Sacks and packs of supplies, saddles, blankets, bridles, and some wooden boxes marked DYNAMITE were jumbled together in no apparent order.

Rogue narrowed his eyes, and looked again and again at every aspect of the disordered camp. No matter how hard he looked, it always remained the same: there was filth, drunken men, and the blazing fire, but nowhere in sight a little girl.

Moving slow and quiet, Rogue eased back down from his vantage point. He had to get closer to the men, to hear what they were saying. Maybe that would tell him what they had done with the child.

He wasn't more than halfway down when a prickling chill stirred the hair on the back of his neck, and he felt doom close in around him. He heard something. Froze momentarily. Right hand inching toward his Colt, he waited, knowing he would kill if he had to, kill every damned one of them, and do it without a bit of remorse.

'Where in the hell are you going?' The hoarse voice came from just below Rogue's rocky perch. The Colt was in Rogue's hand, hammer back and ready.

'I'm just taking that lil' girl some grub,' another man answered drunkenly.

'Forget you ever saw that damned kid,' the first man growled. And it was pretty evident that he had had a swig or two of rotgut himself and was feeling right surly, even before Rogue heard the clang and clatter of a tin plate scraping across stone. 'Get outta here and leave me alone.'

'Now, why'd you wanna do something like that. All that grub wasted. I'm gonna . . . '

The rock still held warmth from the

day's sun, but Rogue was cold, growing colder by the moment, cold with rage, but he held it in check, refused to let it take over his actions, especially when listening would get more results than killing. He twisted around a little and tried to see the two men below him but could only catch a glimpse of moving shadow as they stepped away, moving back toward the fire.

One of them stopped. Rogue knew it was the drunk when the man whined, 'That poor lil' girl, all tied up like that. No grub. No water. Don't it like to tear your heart out?'

'I don't want to do no thinking about that kid,' the other man said. 'The old man said to stay away, and that's just what I aim to do.'

'He's crazy. What he's gonna do to that lil' girl makes me plumb wanna cry.'

'Shut the hell up. I ain't gonna listen to any more of your crap.'

The drunk whispered, just loud enough for Rogue to hear, 'I heard 'em.

The old man and that nephew of his'n. They're gonna hurt her bad.'

'You don't know nothing except how to suck on a bottle.'

'He's gonna heat up his branding iron and put his brand on her lil' face. That's what he said. Then he's gonna cut her tongue out.' Before the words were well out of his mouth, the man began to weep, saying over and over, 'Poor lil' girl.'

'My God, man, you don't know what you're saying. Shut up!' the other man almost screamed. 'Just keep your mouth shut, or we ain't never gonna get out of here alive. You hear what I'm saying?'

'Yeah, but I need whiskey. Lots of whiskey. You got any left?'

'No, but I'll help you find some and take a mighty big swig of it my own self.'

'Poor lil' girl.'

'Yeah, just don't say . . . Dammit, watch where you're going.' The men moved off, stumbling and swearing. Rogue twisted some of the knots out of his tense muscles, returned the Colt to its holster, and crawled down off the rock.

The girl was still alive and likely real close, but Rogue was stymied. It was dark, black dark, and the canyon was probably riddled with holes, shallow caves, and rocky crevices — Faith could be hidden anywhere. There was no way to find her, but he had to and had to do it pretty damned quick. He believed what the drunken outlaw had said. He knew, even without the power that still lingered within him, that the old man, whoever he was, meant to hurt the girl real bad. Rogue couldn't allow it.

Inching along, feeling his way with hands and feet, Rogue made his way toward the north side of the canyon, the wall closest to him. The moon would be up in an hour or so, and while it wouldn't be much help in the bottom of the canyon, it would give a little light. Right now, he needed to find a place to hole-up, and he needed it real sudden like.

Easing his way through the darkness one short step at a time, Rogue was feeling the strain. He stopped for a moment and took in a couple of deep breaths. Before he could move again, he saw a flicker of light off to the left and just a little bit ahead of where he stood. He knew he had to check it out. Maybe it was just another camp guard, but it could be someone standing watch over the child.

Still moving and careful, he headed in that way. He heard something. Stopped. And then, muscles tense and ready for action, he felt his way into a rocky niche and hunkered down.

Someone coughed. Cleared his throat. It had to be the man Rogue was stalking, but whether he was a camp guard or something else, he was a danger and would have to be taken care of — and soon. Assessing the situation, hoping to find some new clue as to Faith's whereabouts, Rogue waited until it seemed like the minutes had grown into hours.

The guard (or whatever he was) shifted, dislodged a shower of stone and sand. A match scratched. Light flared. Rogue could see him plain, and he wasn't more than ten or twelve feet away. He was sitting on the slope of a boulder, hunched forward, lighting a cigarette, one hand lying across the rifle on his knees.

Rogue saw the man, knew the danger, but he had also seen something else in that brief flare of light: the dark mouth of a small cave situated directly behind the outlaw. The girl could be in there — and he had to find out. But first he had to distract the man, take him out of action, and do it without noise.

Reaching down with one hand, Rogue swept his fingers across the ground, searching for small stones. Within seconds he was holding several the size of hen eggs; just right to rattle against the rocks off to the left. If the man was watching the girl, he would have to investigate. Rogue was sure of that, and when he did, Rogue would be ready.

His arm back to pitch the rocks, Rogue froze. Footsteps crunched the gravel behind him. Crowding deeper into the crevice, motionless, Rogue waited for the lantern swinging from the hand of the approaching man to reveal his hiding place to both outlaws. He passed within touching distance on his way to the guard, but the lantern-man didn't even glance in Rogue's direction.

'Where in hell have you been? You planning on starving me to death or something?' the guard said, tossing his cigarette away in an arc of glowing sparks.

'Jake, we ain't got time for eating right now. All hell's busted loose. That damned drunk, Brawles, heard the old man talking to the girl. He got himself a snootful and is crying and talking to beat the band. The rest of that bunch is riled and doing a heap of muttering.'

'Dammit, man, you know I ain't

supposed to budge away from here. Why didn't you just knock him in the head and let him sleep it off?'

'Jake, I'm telling you, them idiots are just about ready to go after the rifles and come up here and take the girl. You've got to do something.'

'They're just drunk. Feed 'em some more rotgut and . . . '

'Jake, you have to come. There ain't nobody going to try to rescue that kid tonight. Before he left, the old man said the girl's pa was down in Eagle Point — him and all his hands. They cain't get back real soon, and there ain't nobody else at the ranch except them two women.'

'I oughta knock your stupid teeth down your throat and . . . '

The man with the lantern whined, 'Now, that ain't no way to talk to me. I did the best I could, and then I came to get you. 'Sides, the old man left you in charge, not me.'

Rifle in his left hand, Jake jumped down from the rock and held out his other hand. 'Give me the damn lantern.'

'I can carry it.'

'Naw, you're gonna stay here and . . . '

'She don't need me. You might. Those drunks are plumb riled — you might need some help. Come on before they start shooting.' He turned and started back toward the camp. The other man followed, swearing loudly. The sounds of their continuing argument hadn't died to a rumble when Rogue stepped out of his hiding place and made a bee-line for the cave.

Barking his shins, stumbling over unseen objects, he felt his way inside and whispered, 'Faith? Faith? If you're in here, don't be afraid. Your brother sent me. I've come to take you out of here.'

His reaching hand touched her head. She sat, propped against a rocky wall, and she neither moved nor spoke. But whatever the devils had done to her, she was still alive — he could feel her trembling as his fingers slid down her tear-wet face until they touched rough cloth. She was gagged, and a second or two later, his hand found her bound wrists — he wanted to untie her, release her from her torment, but there was no time.

'We have to hurry, so I'm going to carry you.' He lifted her carefully. She moaned weakly.

'I don't dare strike a light. Are you hurt?' Rogue felt her nod against his chest. 'Too hurt to go on?' After a very slight hesitation, Faith shook her head.

She didn't weigh much, making her an easy burden for his one hand and arm. He needed the other free to feel his way out of her prison and saw, to his real relief, that the rising moon had poked a sliver of its rim over the canyon wall while he had been inside. He could see a little.

After he scrambled off the rock, he hadn't gone more than three steps when he heard a sound behind him. It was a sound Lejube Rogue knew too well — the sound of a six-gun being cocked.

4

'Turn around slow, you stupid, drunken son-of-a-sow. I wanna see your face when I put a bullet in your cowardly gut. You know what the old man said about touching that kid and . . . '

Rogue recognized the voice, knew the man was the guard, Jake, and went icy, cold to the bone, became what folks had named him: Lejube, a demon without compassion. He turned, drew, thumbed back the hammer, and squeezed the trigger of the Colt in a single, fluid motion.

Jake's answering shot was slower, only the reflex tightening of a dying hand. The powder flare seared the sky, and the man fell heavily, rolled, still twitching, toward the base of one of the towering boulders.

Rogue, the girl held tightly against his shoulder, was already moving when shouts of alarm rent the night. The shouts didn't rowel his hide with sharp spurs. The quiet, the deep ominous quiet that followed, did.

Moving quick and cautious, Rogue carried the little girl up the river, angling toward the canyon's north wall. The camp and the armed men were between him and the deer trail he had used coming in, and he couldn't risk it. He had to find a new way out.

He held the kid as carefully as possible, but he knew he was hurting her. She was shaking violently. Her tears were hot on his shoulder. But she had grit clear through — not even the smallest moan came from her gagged mouth.

'Steady, Faith,' he whispered, trying to make things easier for her. 'Don't cry. Save your strength — you're going to need it by the time we get out of here.' He hugged her a little tighter as he moved away from the cave and into dark pools of moon shadow.

The power that lay within him rose

high, fed his anger. The girl was so small, so helpless, and the outlaws had caused her so much fear and so much pain. They had to pay for that. 'Don't worry, Faith,' he said softly. 'Those men will never touch you again. I will never let them take you back.' And even as he said the words, Rogue knew he had bound himself to a new promise, a promise he would die to keep. His mouth smiled, but not his eyes, and not his heart.

Big and yellow, the moon rose above the trees that fringed the canyon rim, cast its light full on man and child. At that moment, it was both friend and foe, lighting their way to freedom and showing the outlaw gang exactly where they were going.

He gave a mental shrug. It was the breaks of the game, but he still had a few tricks to play and more than a few ways to keep out of sight. Trying to stay in the shadows, he went on, dodging around massive stones; climbing over fallen, vine-tangled logs; pausing to listen for sounds of pursuit; twisting and turning, always searching for a way out of the canyon.

In the wider, gently sloping lower canyon, the river had gurgled and whispered, flowed in almost silence, but as they traveled upward, the canyon floor grew steeper, rougher. The water leaped and roared. Cascading down white-foamed rapids, falling down sheer rock faces. It gave them no safe passage, and the fierce noise almost drowned out the sounds of pursuit. It would have if the men following them had been sober and careful, which, thankfully, they were not.

Rogue could hear them shouting and cursing, discharging revolvers and rifles, shooting at everything and nothing. His own gun in his hand, Rogue walked faster, holding the girl against his sweating body.

They were less than a mile away from the camp when the canyon narrowed still more, forcing them out of the meager shelter the rocks had offered.

Rogue trotted up the muddy trail that lay close to the river's edge — the only course open to him. The granite cliff was practically touching his left elbow, and the river raged at his right, leaving him no other option than to try to get across the open space as quickly as possible.

The cliff curved inward still more, forcing his feet closer to the water. While it had obviously been used by more than one horse, the trail was narrow, wet, and steep. Sweat ran down Rogue's face and soaked his black hair. His breath came in harsh gasps. The child, so light in the beginning, was a leaden weight now, and she seemed to grow heavier with every step he took; but his pace didn't slacken.

Around the long, rocky curve, the trail widened again and wasn't quite as steep. A shallow stream flowed across the track. Rogue splashed through it, heading for the shelter offered by the trees that lay ahead.

The trail led straight into their

shadow, but Rogue and the girl were still in the moonlight when a shot rang out. Lead splatted into the earth just in front of Rogue's feet.

His Colt was ready in his hand, but Rogue was tired. He strained to hold the weapon steady. He couldn't see a thing, but he knew the shot had come from somewhere under the trees.

A mounted man raced out of the darkness, and he was just the first of a pack — Rogue could hear the sounds of other horsemen coming behind the shooter.

Leaning sideways in the saddle, the man shot again. The lead whined passed Rogue, leaving the hot wind of its passage to blow across his cheek. Rogue managed to level the Colt and squeezed the trigger. His shot didn't miss. The man screamed, raised his hands high, and fell into the water; his horse ran on alone.

Rogue doubled back, headed for the small stream he had just crossed. Once in the water, he turned and followed the flow upstream. Somewhere he found enough wind to give the child a whispered reassurance — and enough sense to return his Colt to its holster. 'They're on both sides of us, Faith, so we've got to go where they can't take the horses. I know I can outdistance them on foot. Be brave and hang on a little longer, I promise you we'll make it.'

The icy stream was only four or five feet wide, and its bed was choked with cress, miner's lettuce, and other water weeds that tangled his feet. Slipping on round stones, Rogue fought his way forward, followed the stream through a boggy, willow-grown swamp. Then the creek narrowed, became swifter and deeper. Rogue was soaked to his thighs, and his feet were numb with the water's chill by the time he reached the waterfall pouring down the canyon wall that loomed a hundred feet or more into the night sky.

But, unless the moonlight was deceiving his eyes, there was a way up.

For long years, the creek had pounded its way down the cliff, tearing away slabs of stone, forming a stair-stepped channel of falls and small pools.

Rogue paused, tried to think, to assess the possibilities. He could hear shouts, curses, and occasional gunfire coming from their back trail. Retreat was purely impossible, but the wall in front of him, climbable as it might be, was in full moonlight. The water spilling down its face took the light and magnified it — anyone foolish enough to dare the climb would be totally visible.

Bending his head, he put his mouth close to Faith's ear and said, trying to sound calm and sure, 'It's going to be bad, kid, but climbing is our only chance. Are you with me?' Her answering nod was a little slow in coming, but it wasn't grudging.

Wading through the roiling, swirling pool at the base of the cliff, Rogue started up the treacherous stair. He lifted the girl, sat her on a ledge, and climbed up beside her — and repeated the same action over and over again. Rocks broke beneath his feet. He slid on moss and slick stone, but he moved them steadily up the cliff. It was slow, hard work. The climb took them straight up through the falling water, and they were soaked to the skin before they had gone more than a foot or two.

Faith shivered as he lifted her high, strained to place her on a narrow ledge well above his head. Whether she shivered from cold or fright or both, Rogue didn't know, but he had no breath left to give her any kind of reassurance now. He could only climb doggedly, reach up, lift, slide back, and climb once again — expecting every second to feel the hot burn of lead slamming into his back.

Despite his fears, Rogue and Faith were within reaching distance of the top before the outlaws spotted them and began firing. The first bullet slammed into the stream below Rogue's feet. The second whistled harmlessly overhead.

The third struck a target, scorched a path across Rogue's ribs. Pain or not, he didn't dare stop and examine the damage.

Wincing, he shoved Faith up, dragged his own weary body up after her. Lead splatting around them, the sound of gunshots thundering up from below, he grabbed her, sheltered her with his own bulk, and went up and over the last fall of water. Tumbling together, they rolled into a shallow pool at the top of the cliff.

Out of bullet range, they were safe for the moment, and for the small reprieve, Rogue breathed a heartfelt sigh of relief. Stumbling to his feet, he fished the girl out of the water and carried her to the shore. Sitting her on a grassy bank, he stood silent for a moment, panted for breath, and tried to get his overworked muscles to relax.

After a moment or two, he said, 'Kid, I have to see if they are crawling up the cliff after us. Don't be afraid. I won't be out of your sight. The moon shining full in her face, she looked up at him, and her big, scared-looking eyes seemed to be begging for something, but whatever was bothering her would have to wait. Almost as if she knew that, Faith nodded and looked down at her hands, still bound together, lying limp in her lap.

Rogue drew his Colt, shook the beaded water from its oiled metal, and reloaded the cylinder before he crawled to the brink of the canyon and peeked cautiously over the edge. He could see nothing except the dark of trees and shadows and the shine of the moon-silvered water. There wasn't a hint of movement anywhere. Yet, he could almost feel the men down there, waiting for him to make a false move. Hoping to lure them into making a move, he stood up.

Nothing.

That caused him considerable worry. From the looks and smell of their camp, the outlaws had been holed up in the same place for a long time. It followed that they had had time enough to explore their surroundings, find a better, quicker, way up the wall. Likely they were coming up right then.

Thoughtful, trying to decide their best course, he hurried back to the girl and knelt beside her. Pulling the Green River knife from its sheath in his high-topped moccasins, Rogue carefully cut through the length of rough cloth that held Faith speechless and pulled a wad of the same material from her mouth.

She licked at her dry, cracked lips with a thick, swollen tongue, swallowed hard, and tried to say something. All that came out was a hoarse croaking. She tried again with no better results. Mute and pleading, she held out her bound wrists.

Looking at them, Rogue actually felt his face harden, his eyes turn to ice. The leather thongs around the girl's small wrists had been tied cruelly tight and they had bitten deep. Her tender skin was broken, had bled, was swollen

60

until the thongs were embedded in her flesh.

Anger was cold within him, killing anger. No man had the right to mistreat a child, and this little girl had been treated harshly. Knowing he was going to have to hurt her more, Rogue clenched his teeth and worked the tip of the knife under the leather and began to cut. When the bloody bonds fell away, Faith whimpered deep in her throat. Rogue wasted no time severing the leather that strapped her ankles together and replaced the knife in its sheath.

Being who he was, what he was, and what had been done to him, Lejube Rogue walked alone, and he had no trust, no tenderness, and no love to give to his fellowman — except Eagle Flying. Time, pain, and betrayals had stolen all caring from him. Until this day, he had lived only the promise he had made to his long-dead grandfather.

But something about this little girl, and perhaps her brother, touched him deep. He watched helplessly as she fought a silent battle against the terrible pain of blood returning to her extremities. He wanted to give her ease, comfort, but there was nothing he could say or do. He had been alone too long, he no longer had anything to give.

'Put your hands and feet in the water,' he said at last. 'It's cold enough to numb some of the pain.' He reached down to pick her up, but before he could touch her, she pushed herself forward and toppled, face-first, into the shallow pool. Holding herself up on her elbows, she held her lips to the water's surface and started to drink.

Gulping, barely taking time to gasp in air, she drank until Rogue took her by the shoulders and pulled her up. 'Stop for now,' he said. 'Too much might make you sick.'

'Sorry. They wouldn't . . . ' Her words came in fits and starts, like she was unused to words or maybe her mouth wasn't working right yet.

'Yeah, I know,' Rogue said, hunkering

down so he would be at her level. 'Are you hurt bad anyplace?'

'My wrists are . . . No, I . . . Mister, they killed Robby.' Her skinny shoulders shook with the force of her grief, but she still didn't cry.

'Who's Robby?'

'My . . . my brother. They shot . . . No reason. He fell. Blood and . . . He's dead, mister.'

'No, Faith, he isn't,' Rogue said quietly. 'He was shot in the leg. I found him and did some doctoring. He's still hurting some, but I reckon he's going to make it.'

There was wonder in her voice when she asked, 'Truly, you saved Robby, too?'

'Yeah, I reckon I did. I've got him stashed in a safe place, and we'll be heading there ourselves as soon as we can.'

'Mister, I don't know what . . . Thank you.' She smiled at him, a smile that fought its way through cracked, swollen lips and was real.

Rogue smiled in return. 'Forget it,' he said, and he wasn't real ashamed of the gruffness in his voice, but he wasted no time changing the subject under discussion. 'Kid, I know you're still hurting, but we best be getting before they track us down.'

'I don't know why they . . . That man, he was awful. All hunched over and crawly looking, like a big ugly spider. He said he was going to brand my face and . . . '

'He won't touch you again, and nobody's going to brand you. I'll make sure of that.'

'That old man is crazy. Real crazy. He . . . '

'No more talking. Come on. Let's go find someplace we can hole up until daylight.'

Helping her to her feet, Rogue watched as she took a step. He saw her grimace and asked, 'Do you want me to carry you until your ankles get to feeling better?'

'Mister, I may be little, but I'm not a

baby. I'm seven, almost eight, and I can walk.'

Opening his mouth to argue with her, Rogue stopped before he even started. He saw her pride and knew it wouldn't be right to take any of it away. 'Come on then.'

He turned and started across the small stream, still heading up the canyon rim.

'Mister,' she called softly.

He stopped, looked back.

'Would it be . . . I mean . . . can I hold your hand? It's sort of dark under those trees and . . . '

'Sounds like a real good plan. We won't get separated and have to spend time looking for each other.' He turned, waited until she had reached his side, and when they walked on her small hand was warm inside his far larger one.

5

The first gray light of dawn found them far up the canyon rim, hidden beneath the low-hanging branches of a large hemlock tree. They had walked until the child, stumbling with exhaustion, could walk no more. Now she lay wrapped warmly in Rogue's buckskin shirt and slept fitfully. Ignoring the chilly nip of the mountain air, Rogue sat beside her as he had throughout the night.

Twice during Rogue's vigil, the killers from the canyon had come close. Twice Rogue had drawn his twin Colts, ready to kill to defend the girl. The men, cursing the mountains, the fugitives, and their own weariness, had ridden near — within feet the second time — but they hadn't seen Rogue and Faith. That had been pure luck, and Rogue knew the coming light would reveal them to even the blindest of searchers.

She was plumb tuckered-out, and he hated to wake her, but he had no choice. He touched her on the shoulder, whispered, 'Faith.'

She stirred, groaned sleepily, yawned, sat up, and winced at the pain waking brought her. She looked around, blankly at first, and then fearfully as memory returned. 'Are they coming?' she mumbled through swollen lips.

'Not yet, but we have to get out of here — it's too exposed. Besides, we need to find a way to get to the other side of the canyon and to find a place to hide you while I go for help.'

'Where Robby is?'

Rogue wanted to tell her yes, that soon she would be with her brother, but he couldn't lie to her. 'He's safe, kid, but he's too far away. I'm afraid we're going to need help real soon, and the only way I know to get it is to go after it. So, do you have any idea where we are or how close help might be?'

She sighed. 'No. I think those men took me into South Fork Canyon, but I don't know for sure. Papa thinks girls should stay home and help with the house. Sometimes Robby takes me to look for berries or . . . Papa was gone and we . . . ' She licked at her lips, looked at Rogue, and said, almost tearfully, 'I'm sorry, mister. I didn't mean to cause any trouble.'

'What's to be sorry about?' Rogue asked gently. 'I don't know where we are either. Come on. Let's find a way across and then we can worry about where we are. Okay?'

Nodding, she tried to stretch her battered mouth into a smile. When it didn't happen, she reached up a hand and touched her lips. Rogue got his first good look at her wrists. They were swollen, the cuts made by the thongs inflamed, and in places still seeping blood.

Anger almost stole Rogue's breath, but he steeled himself against its grip. Anger wouldn't get them anything but dead. He did all he could do at the moment, ignored her wounds and asked, 'Are you ready?'

'You better take your shirt.' She skinned it off and handed it to him.

'Thanks.' Taking it from her, Rogue crawled out from under the stiff-needled tree limbs. Standing in dry grass and huckleberry brush, he stretched, twisting and turning, to ease the kinks out of his body. The bullet graze on his ribs stung and bled a little from the exercise.

Faith followed him into the glade and made an almost soundless exclamation of dismay before she whispered, 'They shot you. I didn't know. Why didn't you say something?'

It had been a long time since anybody fussed over his well-being, if anyone ever had, and the little girl's concern warmed him. 'It's nothing.'

'It's bleeding.'

'It's only a scratch, and a little scratch never hurt anybody.' He jerked the shirt over his head, pulled it down, and unbuckled his gunbelts to get the tail of the shirt down around his hips. That done to his satisfaction, Rogue donned the belts, checked the Colts, and said, 'Come on, kid, let's get for getting.'

Leading the way around a moss-grown windfall, Rogue stepped across a tiny stream. The outlaws had forded it twice during the night. Their horses' iron-shod hooves had torn the banks, leaving mud clods, water-filled hoof-prints, and crushed strawberry plants.

Figuring the kid was already spooked enough, Rogue said nothing, but she saw the signs and knew them for what they were. Her blue eyes darkened with fear. 'They came . . . They came that close to us?'

'Does it matter? They didn't find us, did they?'

'No, but . . . '

'No more talking. Sound carries. Just remember, they'll never touch you while I've got breath in my body. I promise you, Faith, they will never take

70

you back,' Rogue said. He knew he had turned into the demon folks named him. But he also knew that demon would die to protect what he claimed as his own, and it seemed he had done just exactly that: claimed one brave little girl.

She swallowed hard before she reached out, took his hand, and gave it a quick squeeze. She said nothing more, and the fear was gone from her eyes.

The sun had climbed high and blazed hot before they found a place that might be a way back into the steep-walled canyon. If they could get down, the other side looked climbable, even for Faith.

Pushing through a screen of young trees and brush, they came out into a small open space. Long ago, floods of rain and melting snow had cut a gully deep into the hillside, and the force of the flooding had loosened the earth and torn an outlet into the canyon rim. Boulders and red dirt had slid from the hillside, fell from their own weight, and dropped down into the canyon. Now, the heaped dirt and stone rested, uneasily, in a great tumbled pile. The canyon walls bulged out on both sides of the slide, hiding what lay below.

Time had tried to repair some of the damage. Blackberry vines and low brush masked some of the earth's scars, and they also concealed the dangers inherent in the slide.

Belly-down on the rocky cliff top, Rogue tried to see where the vast slide ended, but he could see nothing. The prickles raising the hair on the back of his neck were telling him it was too easy. It had the smell and feel of a trap. Getting to his feet, he scouted around, checked the gully for hoofprints. There was no apparent sign to show the outlaws had ever been there.

He hesitated a minute before he said, 'Kid, I'm going down a little ways. Wait for me right here.'

'I will, but I'm kind of hungry. Is it

all right if I eat some of these blackberries?'

Even as he nodded, Rogue felt a quick pang of remorse for not trying to find something for her to eat. He doubted that she would find even a handful of berries. There were many vines, but the berries were sun-blasted, dried around their own seeds. There was none of the cool dampness of the canyon up here. This south slope was hot, and the blackberry crop was almost gone.

'Keep your eyes open and be careful,' Rogue said as he eased down the unstable slope. He moved as rapidly as possible, but he hadn't gone more than thirty feet when he heard Faith's terrified scream.

Dirt and rocks slid under his moccasins as he turned, sending up a cloud of reddish dust. He fell to his knees. Scrambled up. Lunged forward. Fell again. Clawed and grabbed his way upward. Came over the rim like a charging grizzly.

Eyes narrow. Fury turning him to ice. He saw a man with a drawn gun pointed at his chest. Drew both Colts and fired only one. Blood and bone flew from the outlaw's bearded jaw. The man's gun fell as he pitched forward, writhing in pain, choking on his own blood.

'Take him alive! The old man wants him!' someone shouted.

A gun butt slammed against Rogue's skull, just above the bridge of his nose. Blood roared in his ears. His legs went weak. He fell, rolled toward his attacker.

The man's sharp-toed boot drove into Rogue's ribs. Red pain flashed across his chest. He gasped, fought the agony that threatened to engulf him. His left Colt thundered. The man above him clutched at his bloody chest and crumpled down, dead before he was on the ground.

Rogue got to his feet real slow. Faced the yellow cur who held Faith before him as a shield. Moved toward him.

74

'Stop right there! I'll put a bullet in her head, I swear I will!' the man shouted, his voice high, shrill with pure fear.

The fear was justified. Rogue kept on walking.

'Stop, you bastard! Stop! I'll kill her.'

'She's better dead than with you. You put your hands on her. I'm going to make you pay for that,' Rogue said, meaning every icy word. He took another step forward.

The man threw Faith to one side, clawed madly at his still-holstered gun.

Rogue paused long enough to toss one of the Colts he held to Faith. 'Here, kid,' he said. 'Shoot to kill.'

He holstered his other gun, took a single step forward, and his balled fist slammed hard into the man's belly, making a heavy, meaty sound.

The man's hands flew up, and he took a step back.

Rogue followed. Hit him on the point of the jaw.

The outlaw landed on his rear,

bounced, and scuttled away like a frightened spider. Rogue followed, jerked him to his feet. Hit him again and again. The man went down.

Squealing at the top of his voice like a pig about to be butchered, the man got to his feet and tore his six-shooter from its holster. Stepped back. Brought up the gun. A blackberry briar whipped around his ankle. He jerked his foot. Stumbled to one side. Stumbled again. Teetered. Fell over the edge of the rock bluff. His gun discharged on the way down. The sound of the shot and his final scream blended and echoed in the depths of the canyon.

Only one outlaw was left alive. He stood, hands empty and raised high above his head. 'My God,' he said, 'I ain't never seen the like in . . . Mister, who are you?'

Blinking away the blood that was pouring out of the rapidly swelling cut above his eye, Rogue made no answer. His only thought was for the little girl.

She was crouched in the vines where

the outlaw had thrown her. The sharp briars had scratched her arms and one cheek, but there were no tears in her blue eyes. Her face was pale, but determined above the Colt she gripped in her two hands. The gun's black muzzle was pointed at the outlaw's chest, and the hammer was cocked. The gun was rock-steady, and she had two fingers curled around the trigger.

'Should I shoot him now?' she asked.

'Please, mister, don't let her kill me. Honest, mister, I wanted to run when I found out what the old man was . . . But, Slim, he wanted to stay until we got the gold. I should-a gone by myself. I should-a.'

Bent toward the grinding pain in his ribs, Rogue asked, 'Why'd you shoot the boy and steal Faith?'

'The old man did it. I don't know why, and, mister, that's the God's honest truth.'

'You were riding with him.'

'But, I didn't know. The old man was up in Bend, hiring hands. Me and Slim was saddle pards and . . . Mister, we was dead broke and needing a job real bad. The old man said outlaws had killed his brothers, shot him up bad, and stole his ranch. We was supposed to be helping him get what was rightly his. But, dammit, we didn't know he was crazy, crazy enough to shoot his own men if they took a notion to leave.'

The man swallowed hard, lifted his chin a fraction, and went on. 'I ain't usually no coward, but I swear I was afraid to stay and afraid to run. I reckon I ain't much of anything rightly, but I don't hurt little girls.'

Rogue watched the man through slitted eyes, saw the frayed shirt, the run-over boots, and the steady gray eyes that didn't shift before his search stare. He asked, 'Where's Slim now?'

'Down in the canyon somewheres. They split us up, but I gotta tell you that they're down there, waiting for you. They aim to take you alive if they can, but if you put up too much of a fight, they'll just drill you and take the girl.'

'If they can,' Rogue said, his voice sounding every bit as grim as he felt. Turning away from the man, he looked at Faith, smiled a little, and said, 'Thanks, kid. Do you know how to let the hammer down?'

'Robby taught me,' she said. 'What about him?'

'Kale is going back to Bend or someplace else and traveling fast. Right, Kale?'

'Whatever you . . . How did you know my name? Who the hell are you?' Kale asked, just before he mouthed the words that might have been, '*Lejube Rogue.*'

He couldn't have known Rogue had heard him arguing with Slim the day before on the other side of the canyon. But, judging from the sudden change in his voice, he did know the white Indian, the demon who killed without compassion or mercy, bore a real close resemblance to Rogue. And that scared him more than any mortal ought to be scared.

Rogue turned his head, looked at Kale. The man bowed his head, scuffed at the dirt with the toe of his boot, and could not, or would not, meet Rogue's eyes.

'So,' Rogue said, 'now you know me?' He reached in his pants pocket, pulled out a small, heavy leather pouch. 'Here,' he said, tossing it to the other man, 'you'll need this until you can get on your feet.'

'What is it?'

'Gold.'

'But I can't . . . '

'Take off. Now!'

'Yes, sir. But, I'll remember and . . . ' Kale ran for the brush and within seconds they heard his horse crashing through the undergrowth, heading due north.

Faith opened her mouth to say something, but Rogue stopped her. 'Kid, we don't have time to argue, so hike out those vines, and let's get going

80

before some more of them show up.' He wiped some of the drying blood away from his face, felt the wound gingerly. The cut was small, and the swelling was holding it shut, so he couldn't waste time worrying about it.

With her close at his back, Rogue edged and slipped his way down the slide. The great avalanche of earth and rocks had uprooted trees, torn boulders loose, and shoved the whole mess ahead of it into the water, building a tangled bridge of logs and brush across the swift river.

White-foamed water licking at their feet, they stumbled, swayed, and occasionally crawled across the shaking logs. It wasn't an easy trip. Rogue was breathing in short, shallow gasps and bent forward to ease the pain in his rib by the time they reached the far shore.

Faith watched him with worry plain in her eyes, but she didn't say a word. She had tucked the Colt into the sash of her dirty gingham dress, leaving both hands free for their journey. She took it out and tried to hand it to Rogue.

He shook his head. 'Keep it. They're here somewhere. Remember, if you have to shoot, shoot to kill.'

She nodded.

Hoping and praying the outlaws were far behind them, somewhere way down the canyon, Rogue set their course upriver. The prayers weren't answered, and the hope had no basis in fact.

6

Rounding a rocky outcropping, Rogue scanned the area, saw what he did not want to see. A flicker of movement, high up on the broken wall, a flash of light reflecting from a rifle barrel.

'Back up,' he whispered. 'They're up ahead, waiting for us.' Hugging the wall, they retraced their steps, and saw more men down the canyon, coming toward them slow and careful.

'I'm s-s-scared, mister. W-w-we're trapped. Don't let them get me. Please!' The kid's face was dead-white except for the amber freckles scattered across her nose, and her blue eyes were almost black with fear, but she had managed to draw the Colt and was holding it with both hands.

Rogue wasn't ready to admit defeat. He looked hard, examined every tree, every stone, looking for a way out of

83

their current trouble — and finally saw something that might give them an edge, a respite — or maybe escape. 'Kid, we're not licked yet. Look!' He pointed at something a short way down the canyon.

'I don't see anything.'

'A side canyon. See it?'

She nodded, and Rogue began to hurry toward a rock-filled draw that angled steeply away from the larger canyon they were now in. Finally, he scooped her up, ran another yard or two, and tossed her up onto the massive boulder that blocked the mouth of the draw.

He had no choice, but Rogue knew it wasn't the best move, considering the shape he was in. Gasping at the stab of pain in his side, he jumped, clutched a projecting knob of stone, and heaved himself up beside the shivering girl. She stood looking at their back trail, the Colt ready to fire.

'Let down the hammer, kid, and put it away. We're safe for a little while

— they can't do much straight shooting as long as we're dodging in and out of these rocks.' They slithered down the backside of the huge boulder and trudged up a twisting, turning, narrow, dry creek bed that was choked with large and small stones and wiggled around like a snake with a death wound. They were both out of breath but nearing the top when Rogue stopped to listen.

Sweat dripping down his face, his heart already pounding too hard, Rogue added another set of worries to what was already a sackful. 'Hear that?' he whispered, nodding toward the upper end of the gully.

'They're coming down?' she asked.

'Sounds like it,' Rogue admitted, looking around, taking stock — not that there was much to take. The way he saw it, they could go back and get shot, go forward and get shot, or try climbing the wall of the ravine. It wasn't a good choice, but . . . 'Kid,' he said, 'we're going to have to climb.

Think you can do it?'

There was no hesitation in her answer. 'It's not very far. Look, over there. We can go right up.'

Rogue doubted that, but he knew they had to try. They walked over and wasted little time looking. Rock had broken loose in flat layers and left a series of ledges that led up to a steep, grass-covered slope. Refusing to give in to the pain in his ribs, Rogue lifted her up as high as he could and held her until she had a firm grip on the rough stone.

'Don't look down,' he said. 'I'll help you as much as I can, but whatever happens, don't stop.'

She didn't answer, just started inching her way up the wall of stone, going slowly and carefully — too slowly for Rogue's peace of mind, but he followed where she led.

Before they had gone more than twenty feet, a shout came from below. 'They're climbing the damned wall. Go around. Cut them off at the top. Shoot that son . . . ' The rest of the words were lost in the thunder of rifle fire.

She slowed.

'Don't stop! Keep going!' He braced his legs and pushed her hard, shoved her up and over the last of the rock face. She fell, spread-eagle, on the dried grass, wiggled behind a small bush, and crawled on up the slope.

Rogue pulled himself up behind her, hung for a second on the edge. Lead, hot and burning, slammed into his back, knocking him forward onto the grass.

The kid's scream was high, shrill, filled too full of pure terror.

'Keep going! Don't you dare stop!' The bullet had taken him high in the right shoulder, blood ran hot down his back, but it meant nothing. The power was in him. Lejube Rogue was beyond pain, beyond fear. He stood, walked up the slope. Lead splatted and whined around him, but none came close enough to cause him harm. Still walking, he followed Faith through the stand of pine trees at the top of the slope and out into the meadow beyond where she was waiting.

The Colt was still in her hands, and she was looking back, trying to see behind him. 'Are they coming?'

'Not yet, but they will.'

She stepped around behind him, looked at his back.

'You're bleeding really bad. Can you keep going?'

Rogue nodded. 'Head for those rocks. We'll make our stand there.'

They stumbled across the meadow, climbed into the center of a pile of rocks, and got there none too soon.

The power that sustained him was still within him, but his body was growing weaker, his movements slower. Rogue blinked as a ricocheting slug tore dust and sharp-edged chips from the gray rock in front of him. He tried to squirm deeper into the shelter of a narrow crevice, and even that small movement bathed his face with sweat. The stabbing pain in his ribs and the loss of blood from his back drained him of strength, made his gun hand tremble. Blood dripped and dried on the rocks, and his death chant rose in his throat. He kept it there, but Rogue knew that any man, no matter how strong, could die.

The shallow stream that made a half-circle around the base of the pile of stones and the strip of green meadow at its banks wavered, darkened to his seeing. He felt, if vaguely, a cut at the corner of his mouth begin to bleed when he muttered, unable to keep the words from spilling out, 'Lejube? A demon. A demon with a gun. That's what they call me. I have seen the fear that grows in their eyes. I have . . . '

The harsh rasp of his own voice pulled him back from the blackness that waited to engulf him, and he swallowed, or tried to — his mouth was too dry to be much help.

'Mr. Rogue,' Faith asked, 'are they coming now?'

'Not yet. But I reckon they know I

took a bullet when we climbed out of the canyon. Right now, they're just waiting, but they'll come before too long. You can count on that.'

Rogue didn't turn to look at her, he didn't have to. He knew she was there beside him in the pile of tumbled boulders, freckled, dirty, hands and knees raw from the climb, the Colt gripped tight in both of her hands. Rogue felt a new pain — one he hadn't felt in a very long time, if ever. He had felt the omens, sang his death song, and was ready, but she was just a skinny little kid, too damned young to die.

Again the darkness crept in around him; he fought it off, refusing to allow himself to fall. He couldn't. Men waited in the blur of trees just across the narrow strip of meadow. They were vicious, depraved men who would stop at nothing — their acts had already proved the truth of that.

He could hear their horses, knew they would be riding out soon, riding with guns blazing and death in their black hearts. And here he would meet them, Faith at his side, and here they would die — and they would not die alone.

The kid drew in a shuddery breath.

'Scared?' Rogue asked, knowing it was a foolish question but asking it anyway.

'Not of dying. Mister, you know what they were going to do and . . . They will . . . That old man, he wants to hurt me. Please, don't . . . '

'I will never let them have you, Faith.'

'Thank you,' she whispered.

Rogue didn't answer. All that needed saying had been said. She would die at his own hand, die quick and clean, before he would let that crazy old devil get his hands on her.

A dry branch snapped somewhere up in the trees beyond the far side of the meadow, and Rogue thought he heard a stifled oath, both more than enough to start the danger prickles crawling up the back of his neck. 'Kid,' he said, 'I think they've split up and some of them

91

are trying to sneak up behind us. Be ready.'

Following his own advice, Rogue inched back down the slanting rock and tried to turn to face the new enemies. Lead whined and snarled over the rock pile, slammed into stone, gouged furrows in the red volcanic earth.

'They're coming across from the canyon,' the kid shouted, and Rogue heard the deafening sound of a Colt as she fired at the outlaws.

Rogue gripped the boulder with his right hand, steeled himself against the pain, and pulled himself erect. He was a man and would die like one: standing tall, not cowering on his belly.

He stood. Legs spread for balance, swaying just a little, and if death was in his body, it was also in his left hand. He did not intend to die without a fight.

Five men, screaming, spurring their horses, exploded out of the trees, galloped toward the pile of stone, shooting as they came.

Steadying his Colt on the rocks, Rogue squeezed off one shot. Red blossomed on a bearded outlaw's flannel shirt. His blood fouled the stream when he fell. Rogue aimed at a new target. Shot. Another man died.

Something hot hammered its way into his thigh, knocking him sideways. Helpless against the force of the blow, he fell heavily, landed on unforgiving stone. His breath gusted out, leaving him nearly senseless. The roaring in his ears was almost deafening, but still Rogue could hear the shots, knew they were coming from all around them.

They were surrounded — it would have to end soon. He gasped for breath, almost sobbing from the slash of red pain that came with the breath, and struggled to his feet.

The kid screamed. Her Colt roared. Rogue shot at the same time. Two men fell. One cursing and moaning with pain. One with a black-rimmed hole between his staring eyes.

The fifth man lifted his revolver, shot

once more. He looked at Rogue and Faith, beyond them, turned his horse, whipped it with the ends of his reins, and high-tailed it down the small stream as fast as his lathered mount could travel.

More riders, yelling at the tops of their voices, tore down the slope on the far side of the meadow. Carefully, painfully, Rogue turned to face the new enemy. It was almost beyond his doing, but he brought the six-gun up. Slowly, he thumbed back the hammer. He knew he had to make every shot count. He couldn't reload. Three cartridges were left. That made enough bullets for two of the outlaws, one for Faith.

'No, mister. No! Don't shoot!' the girl screeched.

Rogue could hear her, but what she said just plain didn't make sense. Pain had taken all else from him. All he had left was three bullets and the knowledge that he had to kill.

His forefinger tightened around the trigger.

Her little body hurtled across the space that separated them and crashed into his knees. His wounded leg crumpled. He fell and fell hard, but his Colt was still pointed straight at the approaching riders.

Like some small fury, she pounced on him, grabbed the gun, twisted it from his cold fingers. 'You can't shoot. It's Papa. He's found us. We're safe.'

It took a long time, but Faith's words finally penetrated the pain-haze that clouded Rogue's mind. He sighed and relaxed, ready to let the blackness rush in and take him. It didn't quite happen. He closed his eyes. The pain caught him, shook him like a mountain lion shakes a rabbit, and flung him toward the waiting darkness, but he wasn't granted even that much relief from reality.

Dimly, as if she were in some far land, he heard Faith greet her father. Heard his rough-voiced concern. Heard shouts, more gunfire.

None of it mattered to him. At that

moment, all he wanted was to sink into that burning sea of pain and forget everything. He started to chant his death song, but his lips were incapable of movement. He was ready to die.

But Faith wouldn't let him go. She pulled at him, crying, 'No, mister, you can't die now. No!'

Rogue moved his head, trying to shake it, but he was too tired, too weak to argue with her. Some of the power still lingered within him, but he had no strength left — it had all poured out with his blood.

'Papa,' she screamed. 'Don't let him die. Please, Papa, help him.'

'Easy, honey, it's going to be all right now. Papa's here,' Rogue heard a deep voice say, and then he felt someone trying to lift him — and knew he weighed too much for any man alone to do that task with ease. The man realized it, too, and wasn't long in calling for help. 'Shorty! Haskins! Give me a hand here. And hurry, he's in a bad way.'

Too weary and weak to even open his

eyes, Rogue still had enough feeling left to know when they picked him up, carried him out of the rocks, and laid him out on the grass beside the stream.

'Man, he's a big 'un, ain't he?' a voice panted.

'He's that, right enough, and he's gonna be a dead 'un real soon,' another voice answered. 'Just look at him. He's been shot plumb to hell.'

The first voice said, 'Hey, Boss, we'd better be doing something real quick iffen you're a-planning on saving him. He's a-bleeding like a stuck hog and laying here real limp.'

'Papa, no. You can't let him die. He saved me. You have to do something. Papa, please,' the kid cried, sounding like she was sobbing, and maybe crying real tears. Rogue almost wanted to weep himself at the pain and caring in her young voice.

Someone else walked close, cast a shadow over Rogue's closed eyelids, and said, 'You'd be better off to just let him die, Boss. That there is Rogue, you

97

know, that ice-eyed gunfighter folks call Lejube Rogue?'

'How do you know, Ben?' one of the two first speakers asked, sounding real put-out, maybe more so than was right for the time, but Rogue couldn't do anything but tuck the bit of oddness away, save it for another time — if there was actually going to be one.

'Shhheee, old man, if it's any of your business, I saw the devil up in Oregon City. Hell, he just gunned down a man and walked away colder than a snake. Let him die — he don't matter none to us. Hell, as far as that goes, I reckon he's worser than any outlaw around.'

'Don't listen to him, Papa,' Faith said, her voice hoarse. 'He does matter. He saved my life. He's a good man, I know he is. Papa, he got shot because of me. You can't just stand around and let him die.' Her pleas died to a whisper, and Rogue could hear her weeping and gulping for breath.

Faith still wasn't safe, Rogue knew that now. There were still a whole gang of outlaws unaccounted for, outlaws that wouldn't balk at doing a lot of killing to get whatever it was the old man wanted. The kid's father had to be warned. Rogue tried to speak, took in a gulp of air, tried again, with no success beyond a small grunt of sound.

7

His eyelids seemed glued shut. His voice had failed him. But Rogue couldn't give up. He might be dying, but he had to warn Faith's father about the danger, danger from a crazy old man and his pack of killers.

Licking his lips, he managed to croak, 'The outlaws will be . . . not all dead. Will come back. Have to go.'

Ben broke in a little too soon, seemed too eager to discredit what Rogue had said. 'Listen to the yellow-bellied coward. They're all dead but one, and I guess we can protect your worthless hide from him.'

'That's enough,' the kid's father said and came over to hunker down beside Rogue. 'Just rest easy for a little while, son, and then we'll do what we can. Shorty's got a fire built and an iron heating. It won't be long.'

'Damn it, Boss, you just don't know what his kind can do. You ain't doing nobody any favors by trying to save him. Why don't you just let . . . '

Faith's father ignored Ben and went on talking to Rogue. 'It doesn't matter who you are or what you've done. You saved my little girl, and I'm in your debt for that. But all that aside, Shorty's going to be doing the doctoring, and he's going to have to hurt you when he digs those bullets out and cauterizes the wound. But my guess is you know what we have to do.'

Rogue managed a nod.

'We didn't bring any whiskey, so you'll be on your own. Now here comes Shorty, so get prepared.'

Wanting to try again, to warn them of the danger, Rogue could only gasp when callused hands lifted him and started peeling off his shirt. The rough, unskilled doctoring that followed drove Rogue into the waiting darkness — and he was more than happy to receive its painless embrace.

* ★ ★ ★

The darkness thinned and became a gray veil separating him from the world, a veil too thin to keep it out. The September sun still beat down on Rogue's face, but whether it was the same day or not, he didn't know — and didn't really care. He burned with a fire hotter than the sun's. His dry, cracked mouth tasted of blood. Swollen almost shut, his eyes itched and felt gummy, and he wanted to scratch at them, but he couldn't move.

Somewhere, far off, he could hear the kid; she was crying, or else trying to keep from it while she was telling her father about the men, what they had done, and what they planned to do. Rogue knew she was hurting with every word and wanted to help her, but at that moment, he couldn't even help himself. All he could do was lie there and listen.

'Please, don't ask me any more,' she sobbed. 'I just want to go home.'

'Soon,' her father said, keeping his voice low and sort of soothing, 'but now, you have to tell me what happened. I need to know.'

'I can't. They're going to come here and . . .'

'Faith,' he said, sounding like he was nearing the end of his rope and about ready to do something drastic, 'stop acting like a baby. Just start at the beginning and tell me what happened. And stop crying. It's over. Whoever they were, the men who were chasing you are dead.'

'No, Papa, they aren't all . . .'

Her father interrupted, said sternly, 'I've had enough. Tell me what happened. I have to know.'

'Yes, Papa,' she said softly. She was silent for a moment and then the disjointed account of her misadventures seemed to pour out of her.

'Robby and I were . . . Daisy wanted some huckleberries for some pies. She sent . . .' Her voice dropped too low for Rogue to hear the rest of her tale, but he had no problem hearing Faith's father's oath and the angry words that followed.

'The rotten bastards. I'll hunt that last devil down and make sure he dies slow, real slow.'

'Papa, please listen. There are a whole lot more men down in that canyon. Mr. Rogue saved me from them, but . . . Oh, Papa, they shot Robby and . . . They shot him, Papa, and he fell and there was blood and . . . '

Her heartbroken cry ripped through Rogue's daze and brought him to full waking. He sighed. He had promised Faith she would be safe, that that crazy old man would never touch her again, and he had to keep that promise — regardless of the cost. And the only way to do that was to make her father listen and believe what Faith had been trying to tell him.

He raised his head, took a shallow, very painful breath, discovered they had bounded his chest and shoulder tight, and almost choked on the smell of burned flesh — his own flesh. He croaked like a dying bullfrog, but someone was close enough to hear the slight sound and came to where he lay.

A man slid an arm under Rogue's shoulder and held a canteen to his lips. 'Just take a sip or two, son.' He allowed Rogue exactly that before he eased him back down to the grass. 'Try and sleep. You took more'n enough punishment to kill Adam's off-ox. Don't try to talk. Just rest easy a mite, and let us take care of you.'

Opening his eyes as far as the swelling would allow, Rogue tried to see the man who spoke, but he was nothing more than a darkness against the bright rays of the westering sun. 'Who?'

'I'm Shorty, son, Shorty Buskirk. I cut you some and got them bullets out. Then I burned you some with a red hot iron to stop the bleeding. I'm feeling a mite tired, and I purely don't have a hankering to fix you up again.'

Rogue wanted to give the man his

thanks, but he only had air to say, 'Call your boss.'

'Son, I plain don't want to do that. He's tired, and he's hurting bad. Faith just told him his boy was shot. He set a store by that boy. Had himself a heap of big plans and all. Robby was a good boy, and . . . It do be a pity, don't it?'

'Call him.'

'Son, I reckon that's just your fever talking. No right-minded man would want to horn in on another man's grief.'

'Now. I have to talk to him.'

'I'll do it, dammit. Just don't get yourself in a snit.' He moved away.

Rogue closed his eyes to shut out the sun's glare, but his mind speeded up. Now he had a lever, one that just might keep Faith from further harm.

A shadow fell across his face. The kid's father asked, 'Did you want something, son?'

'Mister,' Rogue said, choosing his words with care and using everything he had to keep them together and coherent, 'listen to me. Robby isn't dead. I found him — yesterday or the day before, I'm not sure which. He's hurt some and needs help, but he's going to make it. But I'm telling you, you won't make it through the night unless you head out of here real soon. Those outlaws will be coming up . . .'

'My God! What are you trying to do to me? Are you telling the truth?' Before Rogue could shape an answer, the man went on, 'No, it can't be. Robby's horse came home last night. It was covered in blood. We thought a grizzly had got both kids. I knew Robby was dead, he has to be. Nobody could bleed that much and live. What are you trying to pull? What's your stake in this?'

'Boss,' another man — Rogue was sure it was the one named Ben — broke in, 'I told you. I'm betting this snake was in with the gang. He probably shot Robby his own self and is . . . Kill him, Boss. Shoot him down like the cur he is.'

Ignoring the ranting Ben but wondering what was riling him so much, Rogue said, 'You can believe whatever you will, but your son is still alive. Ben has told you who I am, and it's true. And, if you have heard the tales, then you must know that whatever else I have done, no man has ever called me a liar. So believe this: your son is still alive.'

Wearily, wanting to drop back into the blackness and let the rest of the world take care of its own problems, Rogue listened to Faith's father and Ben argue without getting anywhere, dismiss his words, and circle the problem anew. He knew again what he had learned so often in the six years since he had run away from the mission school. No good came of trying to help other men. They only valued what they paid high to get, or what they feared.

He closed his eyes and waited; and then sort of gasped when Faith's father grabbed him by the shoulders and tried to shake him, screaming like a man driven mad by grief, 'If Robby is still alive, where is he? Tell me, damn you. Where is my boy?'

Hurting almost too bad to answer, Rogue said, playing the only card he had left to save the girl. 'This country is new to me, and I reckon all this scrambling around in the dark has got me turned around. But, boost me up on a horse, and I guess I can find him — providing those outlaws don't get us first.'

'Don't pay him no mind, Boss. He's raving. He thinks he's still shooting it out with the rest of his gang. Forget him and ask Faith where they were when Robby got himself shot — if that's what happened. We can find him ourselves and forget this killer,' Ben said, and it seemed to Rogue that the man was pushing it a little far, was showing that he had some stake in what was happening. Just what it might be, Rogue had no notion and purely didn't have the time or energy to worry it.

Faith's father released his hold on

Rogue, letting him fall, with considerable pain, back to his bed on the grass. 'Faith,' he shouted, 'where were you when Robby was shot?'

She sighed and said, real soft, 'On the Indian Trail. Where it turns north, away from Cur Creek.'

Rogue didn't open his eyes, but he recognized Shorty's voice when he spoke his mind. 'Boss, that's more than six miles from here. It'll be dark in an hour or so, we can't . . . '

'We can, and we will. Robby's hurt; I have to get him home. It won't be as bad as you think. I'll take Ben with me, and we'll cut across the south slope of Rustler Peak, take that deer trail we used last fall. The moon's full, so we shouldn't have much trouble seeing.'

Moving around, Faith's father laid out the rest of his orders. 'Shorty, you and Haskins stay here with Faith and . . . and this man. Neither of them is fit to travel. Build up a fire and cook some of the grub we brought, likely they'll be better by morning.'

His voice far colder than he was feeling, Rogue took a deep breath and said, 'I know you don't believe what I've told you about the danger here, but if you want to save your son, you'd better listen to this. I hid the boy. You won't find him without me — I don't leave a trail.'

'Don't be a fool. I know this country like the back of my hand, there's no place you could put him where I can't find him. So, just tell me where you put him and . . .'

He talked on, but Rogue let the words drift by without even trying to catch the sense of them. It was useless to try to talk sense to this man. He was only thinking of his son — but he had a daughter, too, and Rogue had made her a promise. He had to force her father into doing what had to be done if Faith was to be kept safe.

'I won't tell you. I'll lead you, if you take Faith with us. You should know, Robby was shot in the thigh, hurt pretty bad. He might need finding real quick, and you can't even come close to doing that without me.'

'Son, whether you were riding with that gang or not, I reckon I owe you a lot for saving Faith, and maybe I owe you for saving Robby, and because of that debt, I can't let you do this. You'll be safe here, and so will Faith.'

Even before he had finished speaking, Rogue shook his head.

'You're burning up with fever. The ride would finish you off.'

Rogue said, 'You don't have a real choice. The way I see it, it's either me or your son. Will you let Robby die to save my life?'

To give him credit, the man hesitated a long minute before he said, sounding kind of shamed and speaking real soft, 'No, but, I can't let you . . . '

'Just tie me on a horse, and let's get out of here. I don't care much what happens to the rest of you, but I made Faith a promise. One way or another, I'll see it kept — the rest of those outlaws are going to be boiling up out of that canyon real soon, and I will not let a single one of them touch her again.'

'Be careful, Boss,' Ben snarled. 'Don't waste time listening to him. He's likely trying to lead us into a trap or something. I say leave him here to rot and good riddance, the damned lying snake don't deserve no better.'

'Please, Papa,' Faith said, 'don't listen to Ben. You can't just go off and leave us here. You have to take us both — I can ride, really I can.'

Opening his eyes as far as was possible, Rogue tried his best to see what was going on, tried to read the expression on Faith's father's face, but the man was standing between him and the setting sun. Still, he ignored Faith and Ben and concentrated on the man who had the final say. When he spoke, his voice said all that was necessary, told anyone who cared to listen that there was no give in him. 'The horse, mister.'

The kid's father turned away without

answering, and Rogue caught his first glimpse of the man. He was big, almost Rogue's equal in inches, and bulky. Time had grizzled his reddish hair, but he wasn't soft. His broad shoulders were slumped under the weight of what Rogue had given him. He was backed into a corner, forced to make a choice that galled him, but from the looks of him, he was still trying to find another way out, one that wouldn't kill his daughter's rescuer to save his son.

While Rogue watched, Faith took her father by the hand and led him away. They walked down the bank of the tiny stream, talking low.

The sight hurt Rogue deep. He shut his eyes against the sun's burning and tried not to think of the last time he had been rendered this weak, this helpless. He tried hard, but he was too weak to keep the memories from clawing their way back into his mind.

8

Rogue wanted to groan, to close his mind against the swarm of memories, but it was no use. Even if they had happened sixteen years before, they were as strong as if they had just happened.

He didn't know why that should be, but he knew it was Faith and her father who had called the memories back, brought them into such sharp focus. Sixteen years before, Rogue had been a skinny kid, about Faith's age — seven or so. But he had had no loving father to dry his tears — his father had died at a killer's hand long before. Patrick Scanlon, the boy Rogue had been, had only his grandfather.

The two of them had been walking four days and were somewhere west of the Humbolt River. The Nevada Desert had been hot, burning hot, and their water had run out the day before.

'Ya devel-begotten sissy,' Patrick's grandfather had shouted when the boy fell and struggled to get up. Eyes bulging, face red with rage, the old man had whipped him then, whipped him with a bull whip until his back bled — and it wasn't, by far, the first time it had happened.

Nearly unconscious from pain and thirst, Patrick had cried out for his mother, the woman who had left him to the tender mercies of his drunken grandfather when she had run off with Patrick's father's killer. The weak cry was answered by another taste of the whip.

'Yer ma, is it?' the old man had shouted. 'Ya bawling, worthless pup! Yer ma didn't want ya. She never wanted yer pa. If it wasn't fer me, ya'd been dead long ago. Forget her! All ya gotta do is keep yer damned promise!'

Patrick had known what the promise was, had known that the old man wanted him to hunt down and

116

kill the man who had murdered his father. 'Shoot him down like a dog,' his grandfather had screamed, 'shoot Dolph Odom the way he shot yer pa.'

The boy raised his head, licked his lips. The whip rose once more, but it didn't cut into his back. The man coughed, coughed hard, and gave a harsh rattling gasp. He fell, and they lay together on the caked alkali.

'Patrick Scanlon,' the old man whispered with what was almost his dying breath, 'give me your sacred promise. Promise me before God and all the Saints that ya'll kill him just like he killed yer poor pa.'

'Yes, Grandpa, I will,' the little boy had said, gulping out the words between his sobs. The old man had treated him worse than a stray dog for most of his years, at least, those he could remember, but he was all the boy had in the world, and now he was dying. The boy made the promise that would let him die easy — and it was a promise he felt bound to. Rogue sighed.

That promise would just have to wait; the one he had given Faith had to come first.

'Mr. Rogue,' she said, squatting down beside him and touching his arm, banishing the old memories, bringing him back to the pains and problems of the present.

He opened his eyes but could see very little beyond a blur where she was.

'The horses are ready. I . . . Oh, I don't want you to die. Please, just tell Papa where Robby is and . . . '

'Faith, you know why I can't do that.'

'Yes, I . . . I know, but . . . ' She paused and then added, 'Mr. Rogue, Papa is a hard man. Sometimes I think Mama is the only person in the world who matters to him. He just won't listen to me. I tried to tell him about the rest of the outlaws, but . . . Maybe it'd just be easier to stay here and let . . . '

'Faith, we'll make it. The ride's not going to kill me, I won't let it. I have promises to keep, you know that.'

She didn't make a sound, but her tears dropped hot on Rogue's upturned face. She leaned closer, close enough to whisper a warning. 'Papa doesn't trust you. Ben just keeps . . . '

Ben stomped over and snarled, 'Get away from him, Faith,' as he reached down, caught Rogue by the arm, and tried to jerk him up. 'On your feet, killer. And while you're at it, maybe you'd better remember you're not the only one who keeps promises. I'm not a stupid little girl, I know who and what you are, and I'll promise you this: I'm gonna have a gun on you the whole way. Make one false move, I'll blow daylight through you.'

Fighting to remain alert, Rogue bit back a gasp of pain and tried to get a handle on what was happening. Ben wanted him dead, that much was sure, but Rogue didn't know why. As far as he knew, the man was a stranger, a stranger who didn't know a lie from the truth. Or maybe he was just lying about Rogue for some reason of his own.

He wanted to demand an answer but had no breath to spare and no strength to fight. His rescue came from an unexpected source.

'Ah, Ben, just look at you, playing the fool again,' Shorty said, adding what sounded like a good-natured chuckle to maybe ease the bite in his words. 'Boy, I'm a-wondering when you're gonna learn some sense. Take the way you're a-carrying on about this Rogue fella. Why, he ain't got enough strength left to swat a horse-fly iffen it was a-chewing on the end of his nose. Why don't you just leave him be and go over and get that horse we brought in case we found Robby?'

'Damn your black hide, Shorty, leave me be! I talked to the boss about this killer and we ... We're keeping our guns real handy in case ... ' Ben's voice rose a little and his hand tightened on Rogue's arm for a fraction of a second before he released his hold.

Rogue had to close his eyes, to fight back the dizziness that threatened to engulf him, but that didn't stop him from hearing what was being said.

From the sound of things, Shorty wasn't doing any backing away. He said, 'Well, to my way of thinking, you and the boss are being a mite hasty and maybe a-jumping at your own shadows. Rogue saved Miss Faith, and maybe we ought-a be a-thanking him for that, not trying to put more holes in his carcass.'

Ben wasn't long on answering. 'Damn it all to hell, Shorty. You ain't never had no use for me, not even now when I'm telling you he's a bad 'un. He's in with those outlaws, and, by damn, if you had a lick of sense, you'd know it, too.'

'Naw, Ben, I don't reckon I would,' Shorty said. 'They was doing a powerful amount of shooting to kill — now if they was pards, why would they be doing something like that?'

'That don't mean diddly. Trash like that don't have any honor. They'd just as soon shoot each other as anybody else.'

'Ben, I reckon you best pay heed to old Shorty. I don't know much of nothing about no outlaws, and I reckon you don't neither. We ain't had no trouble around here for a time, and the way I's seeing it, this likely ain't much neither.

'Them men that was killed here, they was strangers to these parts, likely just riding through and maybe drinking a mite. They was probably just joshing with the kids and somebody got carried away. They paid for what they done, and like as not, there ain't no real harm been done. Robby took a bullet, and Miss Faith is scared some, but they'll get over it. And, this Rogue now, I figger he just sort-a happened by and took a hand when he saw what was going on.'

'Think what you want, you old fool. I reckon Rogue is the last of them outlaws,' Ben said, 'and, by God, I don't trust him one little bit. He may be a-thinking he's fast with them guns of his, but I'm a-telling you right straight out, there's other men that's faster, and if he messes with me, he's liable to find one real quick.'

It sounded too much like a threat to give Rogue any ease. He opened his eyes and rolled over to his right side. The movement left him breathless, but now he could see three men. Two of them were medium built, medium tall, and medium aged. In their sweat-stained, battered hats; worn, dusty clothes; and run-over boots, they had the look of a thousand other ranch hands, except that one of them, Shorty by the sound of him, was black.

The other man had to be Ben. He was younger, taller, and thinner, and Rogue had seen his kind before, too. His six-guns, tied down and slung low on his hips, were a little too new, his boots bench-made and shiny — a little too shiny. He talked a little too much, and someday, somewhere, someone would either feed him his words or a bullet.

Ben and his kind were dangerous,

mostly because down deep they were cowards, and they knew it. If Ben got a chance, he would do his best to shoot Rogue — in the back if necessary — and then brag about it. Rogue wanted to sigh again, but he didn't.

Shorty, the black wrangler, said, 'Ben, we've ridden together some, and I ain't aiming to have no trouble with you, so just go get the horse so's we can get out of here. I'm real tired, and I'd like to crawl in my bunk some time tonight — iffen that's all right with you.'

Ben stood there dividing his scowl between Shorty and Rogue without making a move to obey Shorty's order until the kid's father, who was somewhere out of Rogue's sight, called impatiently, 'What's the hold-up?'

'It ain't much a nuthin, Boss,' Ben said quickly, and then he said, a whole lot softer and meaner, 'Just remember what I said, Lejube Rogue. I hope you forget and . . . I'd purely like to kill me a demon.'

He strutted away before Rogue could answer, but that didn't matter much to Rogue. He didn't have anything to say to Ben . . . yet.

'Don't pay him no mind, Rogue. Ben's just a mite too big for his britches since the boss made him foreman. He'll grow up, maybe, and learn a few manners, iffen somebody don't shoot him first. I'll tell you right now, it's a mighty tempting thought sometimes,' Shorty said, but there was no anger showing on his face as he stared after Ben; there was only puzzlement leavened with a heaping tablespoon of pure, worrisome trouble.

'Now, you take you. Me and Haskins have heard a powerful amount of tales about Lejube Rogue — and told a few our own selves; they make right good telling. We figger a man is as good as his word until he shows us different. We think you're a-telling the truth the way you see it — and we ain't gonna fault a man for that. What I'm a-trying to say is, we believe you, son. We don't take you for no kind of liar.'

Knowing something was required, Rogue said, 'Thanks, Mr. Buskirk.'

'Shorty, son. Just call me Shorty, that way I know who you're a-talking to,' he said. Then he smiled at Rogue and Haskins, the other puncher, helped Shorty get Rogue to his feet. — His wounded leg trembled with his weight, and he came very close to pitching forward, falling, face-down, back to the dried grass that covered most of the meadow.

Ben led the horse close, and Shorty and Haskins boosted Rogue up like he was a sack of meal, mounted him on a California saddle. All three were doing a goodly bit of sweating and panting before Rogue was astride the horse. He swayed groggily as they stuck his feet in the stirrups, and for more than an instant, the landscape seemed to recede and darken, blurring his sight.

'Here, boy, take a drink of this a-fore you pass out,' Shorty said, pressing a canteen of water into Rogue's hands.

He took a drink, but it didn't help much. What he really needed to do was lie down, maybe sleep for a week or two. But he couldn't. They had to get away and quickly — he was afraid they had wasted too much time already.

He handed the canteen back to Shorty and felt the empty holsters of his gunbelt. 'My Colts,' he said, fully aware of how thick and weak his voice sounded, 'give one to Faith. She needs it — the outlaws will be coming back.'

'She's got it, and here's your other one. It's all wiped dry, reloaded, and ready to go — Faith made real sure I attended to that right proper,' Shorty said. He gave a fond chuckle before he lowered his voice and added, 'Poor little kid, her ma's been sick for a long time, and sometimes I reckon the boss forgets just how little she really is. Sorry, I'm a-talking out of turn, 'specially now when we need to get out here.'

Not wanting to make any comments on Shorty's words, Rogue knew he needed to say something. 'Shorty,' he said, 'I'd hate to ruin your doctoring by falling, so I'd appreciate it if you'd tie me on.'

'Boy, that ain't a job I'm hankering to repeat my own self,' the wrangler said, giving a little chuckle. 'Haskins, I reckon this 'un's up to you.'

The meadow smelled of horse, sweat, blood, and death, and Rogue was anxious to be gone. The horse was restive, shifting from foot to foot, moving sideways, giving Rogue a few jolts of pain along with a clearer view of what had nearly been his last stand. The dead outlaws were gone, presumably buried under the fresh mounds of earth marked with crude crosses, but danger still crawled up his back, told him to get going.

He could only wait. Haskins pulled off his faded neckerchief and bound Rogue's hands, if loosely, to the saddle horn. Rogue nodded his thanks, watched, and listened as Ben rode close, leaned over, and examined the bonds.

'Dammit it all to hell, ain't you got any sense at all? Get a rope, tie his hands tight, and then tie his feet to the stirrups. Ain't no use being so easy — he's a killer and needs to be treated like what he is. Do you hear me, Haskins?'

Haskins looked from Ben to Shorty like he was trying to decide who to obey, but it was the girl's father who had the say-so, and he wasn't long in giving it.

'Good Lord, Ben, you must be really spooked about this, but forget it for now. He isn't a prisoner, the bonds are for his own safety, not anything else. Now, that that's settled, so let's get. Shorty, lead the gelding the boy is riding, and Haskins, you ride beside him. Get ready to grab him if he starts to fall — from the looks of him, it might be real soon.'

The way he was feeling, Rogue wouldn't have disputed anything anyone had to say about his physical condition — he was feeling every one of his wounds, and he knew every step the gelding took was only going to increase the pain.

But all he said to Shorty's questioning look was, 'I'm ready.'

9

They rode out, heading west, straight into the setting sun. Rogue gripped the saddle horn with both hands, closed his swollen eyes, and hung on. They had climbed the grassy slope and entered the trees, and things were a little better — at least he could open his eyes again and try to get some sense of the country they were traveling.

Faith's father rode point with the girl mounted behind him; Ben brought up the rear. Rogue's horse, a big, rangy bay, was a little feisty and showed it by side-stepping and pulling against the lead rope Shorty held. Every dancing step the horse took was a fiery knife stabbing Rogue in the chest. He hunched over, trying to find some relief from the pain.

Haskins rode close enough to pat him on the bare shoulder. 'Just try to relax, likely you got a couple broken ribs. We bound you up tight as we could with that leather shirt of yourn, but it ain't gonna help a heap or a whole lot. Lordy, them things do smart.

'I recollect one time, it must-a been eight, nine years back. No, by doggies, that don't seem right. Well, anyways, I was younger then, and I was a-breaking out a string of wild ones for old man Jacobs. Well, sir, the very first one, a hammer-headed dun, he took out . . . '

'Shut your yap, Haskins,' Ben snarled, his voice louder and meaner-sounding than it should have been. 'Nobody wants to hear a no-account saddle-bum tell a pack of lies. If you're so keen on yarning, why don't you get that white Injun there to tell us about all them innocent men he gunned down — likely more'n half of 'um shot in the back.'

The horses' hoofbeats were muffled, hollow-sounding as they made their way into a dense stand of young fir, but Shorty's voice was firm and clear when he said, 'I reckon that's more'n enough, Ben. Why don't you just hold off until Rogue has healed some before you start getting real proddy?'

They rode without speaking. The miles fell away as they rode slowly, climbing steadily through open timber with a few twists and turns to detour around windfalls and chinquapin thickets. It wasn't really quiet: the forest was alive with sound, but it was peaceful.

The setting sun sent rays of slanty orange light between the tree trunks. Crashing and snapping their way through the brush, deer ran before the horsemen; jays scolded; grouse whirred and fled. Trees creaked and groaned, the wind sighed and whispered, and the horses' bits jingled.

The smells of dust, evergreens, and decaying leaves tickled the inside of Rogue's nose, brought him close to a sneeze. The pain in his shoulder, ribs, and thigh throbbed with every beat of his heart. And yet, perhaps because of the fever that was building high within him, he felt an ease he had not known in years — if ever. He didn't know the cause and didn't really care either but was content to accept the moment.

Darkness came slowly. The Oregon summer evenings were long, slow to die. Faith's father kept them riding at a steady pace until it was nearly full dark. Finally, he drew rein and said, 'We'd better give the horses a breather. You boys help Rogue off the gelding.'

'If it's all the same to you, sir, I'd just as soon stay put,' Rogue gasped. There was no way he could mount the gelding again, and he knew it. He was hurting bad, and he could feel something hot and wet oozing down his back. He hoped it was sweat.

Nobody tried to change his mind. Shorty brought a canteen and offered Rogue a drink. Rogue shook his head. He was light-headed, vomit rose bitter in his throat, his eyes burned, and he was shivering with cold — despite the heat that was growing steadily stronger inside him.

The others drank, walked around, stretched the kinks out of their muscles, but Haskins stayed close to Rogue's bay. After a minute or two, he cleared his throat, spat noisily, and asked, 'Rogue, you know anything about this here mountain we're a-climbing? Like how it got its name and all?'

'No,' Rogue answered, feeling a faint gratitude toward the man. He knew Haskins was talking to take Rogue's mind off the pain, and he welcomed the distraction. 'I'd like knowing,' he said, meaning it.

'Well, sir, about three years ago, no, by dabs, it were two years ago. Yeah, I remember now. It was the fall of '71. I recollect it true because that was the same year that dang range bull charged my horse, knocked us right smack-dab into a big hornet's nest. Lordy, you never seen the like.

'When them hornets came a-boiling out, that fool horse took out a-bucking and a-jumping. I was a-hitting at them with my hat and a-cussing with every

135

breath. Them bald-headed devils was a-buzzing and a-stinging something fierce.

'One of 'em hit me in the back of the neck, and I swear it liked to knocked me off that dang horse's back. In no time, I was swole up like a poisoned pup. Why, boy, you couldn't even see my eyes. Rogue, I purely wasn't no good for a week or more.'

Shorty laughed. 'Haskins Dole, you ain't never been no good, and you know it. Here you go, trying to pull a fast one. Now, Haskins, Rogue is stove up a mite, but he's still got all his sense. He knows as well as I do that you're too damned ornery for any right-thinking hornet to sting. Why, them old boys would just take one look at your ugly mug and run, hollering for their mamas.'

Although no one would consider him a light-hearted man, the easy friendship between the two men made Rogue want to smile. He had never had a close friend, except for Eagle Flying, and that

136

hadn't been an ordinary friendship. Small boys, even if they have the seeds of power within them, do not make friends with men of power. Eagle Flying was that, and more. *Much more.*

Rogue's grandfather hadn't trusted a living soul, and he had taught Rogue well on their long, slow, westward journey. They hadn't stayed in one place more than a couple months. The old man had dragged the boy over most of the western states, following rumors, looking for Dolph Odom, working when he had to, and whipping or crying over young Patrick, depending on how the drink took him.

There had never been any time for making friends, and after the old man's death, Patrick Scanlon had followed new teaching. The teaching of Eagle Flying was hard for the few years it had lasted, but it was also the best time young Patrick had ever spent. It hadn't lasted.

Rogue thought of the Indian shaman, the only person in the world who might care for him, and sighed.

Haskins misunderstood. 'Now, just look what you've gone and done, Shorty. I'm purely ashamed of you. You just ain't got no feeling. You know better than to make a man with busted ribs want to laugh. Hell, man, something like that could do some real serious damage.'

'No,' Rogue was quick to say. 'I'm fine, really. But you didn't tell me how the mountain got its name.' He wanted to keep the two men talking. It helped hold back the foreboding that hovered over him.

Rogue was uneasy and growing more so each passing moment. He hadn't heard a sound from their back trail, yet he knew, regardless of what Faith's father thought, that the outlaws wouldn't let them escape without a fight. The old man, whoever he was, had wanted Faith bad, and Rogue guessed he still did.

'By nab, Rogue, you got me there. I must be a-getting old,' Haskins said. 'I ended up a-telling you a whole different yarn. Well, I reckon I'd better just start again.

'Two years ago, it was. The boss had lost a lot of steers and young stuff that summer. At first, we just thought they was holed up somewheres. This is almighty rough country, not like across the mountains where it's all flatlike and sage-brushy. Anyways, when we started a-rounding up the strays to drive 'um down to the valley, we knew for sure they was gone. Rustled.

'We figgered it was them Butler brothers what done the stealing. They was three of the no-goodest, rottenest skunks that ever walked God's green earth. Why, Rogue, them three'd sooner spit in your eye than say howdy.'

His back ramrod straight and his eyes narrow, Ben stalked over, scowled at Haskins, and said, 'God, what a crock! Old man, iffen I was you, I'd just tell the story or keep my yap shut. As for me, I've got a bellyful of your rambling and lying.'

Shorty did a little talking and some scowling of his own. 'Whoa up there, Ben. It's his story, so let him tell it. We was there, and you wasn't, so leave be.' The wrangler's voice was soft, but it seemed to Rogue that it held a new edge of anger.

The quiet that followed got pretty thick before Haskins cleared his throat and said, 'Yeah, by gollywampus, we was there right enough, and we was the only ones there with the boss.'

'Dammit, I would have been there too iffen the boss hadn't sent me down to J'ville to find that new Injun agent. I don't much like what you're a-saying neither. I ain't ducked out on a fight in my life, and you damn well know it.'

Haskins got real still, looked down, scuffed at the earth with his toe, but Shorty had a few more words to say on the subject. 'Yeah, Ben, I reckon we all know where you was supposed to be, but what I recollect is: you was gone more'n three weeks and came back claiming you couldn't find the agent.'

Ben turned around, looked across the twilight-dark clearing to where Faith and her father were standing. 'Boss,' he said, 'you tell 'um. You know I was doing what you said.'

The growing darkness made seeing real difficult, but Faith's father's words made his position clear. 'Haskins, just tell the story. It doesn't matter where Ben was — it doesn't have anything to do with what happened.'

He might not have been suspicious, but Rogue was. Ben was plainly up to something. Just what, Rogue didn't know. He could understand Ben wanting to shoot-it-out with him — he wasn't the first and probably wouldn't be the last to have that ambition — but why was he trying to force Haskins and Shorty into some kind of showdown? He took in a shallow breath, shivered a little as the danger prickles gave the back of his neck a new warning, and knew that something bad was just waiting to happen. But not what.

He listened to the next exchange of

words, but the worry stayed in his mind.

A sneer unmistakable in his voice, Ben said, 'Get with it, old man, but stick to the facts. Tell us again how you and Shorty saved the steers.'

Seeming unaffected, Haskins started his tale again. 'The boss, Shorty, and me, we was a-chasing cows out of the draws. Now, I don't know if you've ever punched cows in the mountains, but, well, most of the critters have got enough sense to start for lower ground when winter's doing a little threatening, but not all of 'um. Some of them old mossbacks'll hide in the mostest unlikely places.'

He reached out, gave Rogue's knee a pat, and went on, 'Well, sir, we had been a-rousting 'um out for a couple of weeks when we hit this one canyon. Lordy, it was a mess. Slick-sided and filled plumb full of slick leaf. That there brush was so thick you'd a-thought a gnat couldn't have crawled through it, but there was this one old heifer, danged if she hadn't got in there some way. And, by nab, we knew she was in there 'cause she was a-bawling and a-carrying on like a painter had her.

'Boy, we tried to bull our way through that there slick leaf, but all the sweating and cussing in the world couldn't have got us through. We backed out, climbed the side, and rode up the north rim for a ways, a-looking for a way in to fetch that blasted cow.'

Acting like he had a bad case of the fidgets, Ben started pacing and muttering under his breath, but that didn't seem to bother Haskins much. He patted Rogue's knee again and went on, 'We was just about ready to hang the whole thing up when we come onto this here trail. Damned if it didn't lead us straight down to a box, a side canyon off the one we was a-trying to get into. This canyon was as pretty as you please — with a spring, open meadow, and everything. Well, sir, them rustlers must-a thought so too, 'cause there they was, and right busy, too, a-branding a small herd of the boss's lost beef.

'We found our cattle thieves right enough, found their hideout about halfway up this here mountain. Now, boy, I tell you, they didn't take real kindly to being found, so they up and fired off a few rounds in our direction.

'Seeing as how we had cover and they didn't, that was a mite stupid on their part. We answered their fire. There was only seven of them, so we figgered we had the best of the deal

'I tell you, boy, it got right noisy there for a minute or three, but, by nab, we got 'um all — except one and he high-tailed it out of there like a turpentined hound. He was shot up some and a-leaving a blood trail even a college boy could-a followed.

'We strung up the ones that wasn't dead, and the Butler brothers, leastwise two of them, was the first ones to try on them hemp neckties we made for 'um. They whined about it a mite, but, by doggies, them neckties fit real good.

'After we was through with our chores in that there canyon, we set out to trail the other one. We lost him when he took to the water in South Fork. We figgered he must-a died somewheres in the canyon 'cause he was a-bleeding right smart.

'Anyways, that's what happened, and after that folks just naturally started calling this here mountain Rustler Peak after what we did to them rustlers down in that there box canyon.'

The story interested him. He sensed it had more meaning than he knew — and for a moment, Rogue wished he could conjure the power to try to figure what it was he was missing. He hadn't the strength for that, so he asked, 'Didn't you ever find the other brother?'

'Naw,' Haskins said, moving away to remount his horse when Faith's father announced it was time to ride on. 'We dang sure didn't, and it's a dirty shame. Nash Butler was the meanest son-of — 'scuse me, Miss Faith — he was the sorriest pup of a real bad litter. Why, Rogue, a couple of the Butlers even had some boys, and the way I see it, there wasn't a keeper in the whole sorry lot.'

The moon had stuck an edge over the treetops while Haskins was talking, but the pale light didn't do much for the trail they were following. Rogue saw it led into the darkness beneath trees too closely grown to admit light at high noon, and he wanted to shiver with dread. Danger waited, and there wasn't a thing he could do about it.

10

Faith's father mounted and rode out. The rest of them followed him into the inky shadows. Rogue was glad Shorty was leading the gelding because he was far from sure he could have ridden without that aid. The trail and shadows moved and twisted like snakes to his seeing — he reckoned it was from the fever that was burning in him, but knowing the why didn't help. He closed his eyes, swallowed hard, and winced as tree branches slapped his face and shoulders.

Rogue knew he was slipping into a daze, and he hung on to the saddle horn for dear life. But he couldn't keep his battered body from slumping lower and lower over the horse's neck.

'You all right, boy?' Haskins asked. 'It ain't but a mile or so to where we're a-heading. We'll hit Injun Trail above

Cur Creek. Think you can make it that far?'

'Yes.' Rogue ground the single word out from between clenched teeth, knowing that he could only stay on the horse for a short time longer. Pain and weakness were wearing at him, taking power, strength, and resolve — when he was emptied out, he would fall, and that couldn't happen until Robby was found and the two kids were safe off the mountain.

Later — how much later Rogue couldn't have said — he heard Faith say, 'Papa, this is the place. That man shot Robby over there, see? Where the ground's all . . .'

'That's fine, honey,' her father said, 'now, you just wait here and hold the horses while we spread out and find Bobby.'

'Haskins,' Rogue said, his voice coming out in a hoarse whisper, 'tell him, not here. Ride on.'

The cow puncher didn't have to relay the message. Faith's father had heard, muttered something under his breath, and followed Rogue's directions.

Shorty said, 'Stay close to Rogue, Haskins. He ain't gonna make it much further.'

He couldn't straighten up, couldn't open his eyes, could barely breathe, but Rogue found enough strength to say, 'I'll make it.' But he wasn't real sure he was telling the truth.

They traveled on slow. Keeping his voice low, Haskins asked, 'Rogue, are you sure you can find him? I mean, things look a heap different by moonlight, and you're plumb tuckered out.'

The words wouldn't string together and make sentences, but Rogue got them out. 'Meadow. Grass. Huckleberries. Open timber on both sides. Sugar pine snag. Lightning struck. White. Bark gone. Left of trail. Tell me when.'

'Boy, are you sure? I know that there spot, and I'm a-telling you there ain't no place there to hide anything bigger than a pup.'

'Snag,' was all Rogue was able to

gasp out for a minute or two, and then he found enough strength to say, 'Tell me when.' Somehow, he knew he was still in the saddle, hanging on for dear-life. But his thinking was real fuzzy and his mind kept trying to wander off, to find someplace dark where there wasn't any pain or any promises to keep. He wouldn't allow it. The outlaws were near, he knew it, could almost smell them, and now wasn't the time he wanted to meet up with the likes of them.

First, he had to make sure Faith was out of that old man's reach, and then he had to heal some. After that, he would do what needed doing — the old man and his murdering gang of curs would never live to touch Faith again.

The sure knowledge kept him from falling completely into the darkness that waited, but when the gelding stopped, Rogue slid forward, almost falling. 'Outlaws?' he asked.

'No outlaws here. Wake up, boy. You're a-having a bad dream.'

His tongue was too thick, but he managed to say, 'Wake.'

'We're where you said. Yonder's the snag. Where's Robby?'

'Fir thicket.'

'Lordy, Rogue, there ain't . . . '

Remembering his precautions, Rogue interrupted. 'Left my Spencer carbine. Yell before you ride in.' That small effort exhausted him, but weary as he was, he couldn't stop listening to the reunion that was taking place — nor could he stop the danger warning that was doing its little dance on the back of his neck.

It sounded like Robby's pa was getting in a few licks. He was scolding the boy for taking his little sister into danger, reminding the boy of his mother's illness, and telling him what his acts had cost her. Then the voices faded, to Rogue's hearing anyway, and were lost. Rogue thought the rest of the group rode out to where Robby and his father was arguing, but he wasn't sure.

All he really knew was that he was

alone on the trail, almost lost in some fevered daze, when he heard a horse whicker. It was close, too close, and it fairly screamed of danger.

Rogue pulled against the bindings that held his wrists, jerking at the kerchief, trying to free himself. Pain raged through him. Bitter vomit rose in his throat. His hands came free. Unable to do anything else, he leaned forward and gagged.

Powder fired. Lead whined over his bent back. The bay jumped. Rogue fell, hit the cindery earth, and felt the power return, drag him into some other place, made him listen to a voice from long ago and far away. Or perhaps he walked in a dream, one sent by an old shaman.

'Go deep, little brother, go deep into the stillness of yourself. Go deep, and wait for the healing. It will come,' Eagle Flying said, speaking the same words to the man that he had spoken to Patrick Scanlon. The boy he had found, beaten, bloody, lying beside a dead man, four-days out in the desert.

The old shaman was inside Rogue's mind, plain as day, and Rogue said, although no sound passed his lips, 'I know it's only a dream, Eagle Flying, but I give you welcome. I would do as you say if I could. I'm hurt bad, maybe dying, but there's no stillness in me, not any more.'

The image of the old shaman moved, seemed to take on a look of sadness, but there was nothing of sadness in his voice when he said, 'Ah, little brother, once I dreamed a dream of seeing. Following its teachings, I rode out into the heat of the desert. You were there, waiting, as the dream had told me. It was a true dream.'

Rogue bowed his head, if only in his thoughts, looked down, not daring to meet the wise old eyes that searched his face, and his voice held only shame when he confessed. 'My dreams have all turned to nightmares. Waking or sleeping, I am a demon. Patrick Scanlon is gone, now I am only Lejube Rogue, the demon who rides alone.' He sighed, wanted to say more, but couldn't.

Someone pulled at him, tried to lift him. The dream fled. Rogue tried to fight off the man who tortured him. He kicked with his good leg, lashed out with his fists, and came to just enough to hear Haskins say, 'By nab, would you look at that. I ain't never seen the like in my life.'

Ben's anger came in clearer. 'You wouldn't be so damned admiring if he smacked you in the eye. And, you'll be doing a different kind of laughing when I get him for this — and I damned sure will. Ain't a man born that can punch me and get away with it.'

'Mr. Rogue doesn't know what he's doing,' a girl's voice said. Faith put her hand on his cheek and said, 'Mr. Rogue, can you hear me?'

He opened his eyes, closed them just as quick. There wasn't anything to see except a whole lot swirling dark that made him dizzier just to try and look at. 'Faith? Did they . . . Are you . . . '

'Don't talk,' she ordered. 'Don't

fight. They're just trying to help you. Do you understand?'

He understood all right, but there were a few things he needed to know before he allowed much more to happen. 'The outlaws?'

'They're gone. Mr. Rogue, please, they have to get you back on the horse.'

Her voice was full of worry, but Rogue couldn't ease it yet. 'They shot. Where's my gun?'

'Listen to me. You're burning up with fever and your shoulder is bleeding again. I don't want you to die. I don't want . . . ' Her voice was lost to a sob.

'Don't cry for me. Promise. Don't cry.'

'I promise, now let the men . . . ' Her voice trailed away and was lost as hands slid under him, lifted him up, and dumped him, face down, across a saddle. Pain jolted through him, too much pain, and his knowing again fled to where Eagle Flying waited.

The man of power led Rogue into a swirl of red mist. Together they walked past unseen men who gasped for breath and made plans to ride out, head for the ranch. And then the men were gone, and Rogue followed Eagle Flying out into the heated air of a desert summer.

Somewhere within him, Rogue knew it wasn't true, that he was only dreaming, but he knew only joy when the old Indian, a smile crinkling the skin around his deep-set eyes, put his hands on Rogue's shoulders and said, 'Little brother, I give you welcome. My heart knows only happiness at your return.'

'I know I dream, Eagle Flying, but it is a good dream.'

'Ah, you have forgotten. But, you are still young, and the young must always find their own way back to knowing. Dreams led me to you once, why cannot this be true also?'

'Too much has happened since you gave me to the black robes. They gave me teaching, white man's teaching, from books and tongue, and they ordered me to believe their truth. They took the teaching you gave me and turned it into feathers and smoke.'

Eagle Flying leaned close, looked deep into Rogue's eyes, 'Little brother, are you at one with yourself and the earth?'

'No.'

'Do you believe the black robes' truth?'

'No.'

'Did you forget me?'

'Never that.'

'Ah,' Eagle Flying murmured, leaning closer still, so close that all Rogue could see was the deep brown of his eyes. All he could hear was the shaman's deep soothing tones as he said, 'The boy believed in me, little brother, believed me and gave me love and trust.'

'You let them take him away. You sent him back to the world he had always known. You sent him back to hate, pain, and killing. You destroyed his trust.'

'Little brother, your words are harsh with truth, but it had to be. They came for him, and I had to let them take him. He wasn't free to stay; he was bound by the vow he had made to his grandfather. It sat heavy upon his soul. I could not take that from him; he had to find his own way to freedom. I could only hope for his return. He was a good boy, little brother, and he had much of the power.'

Rogue met the old man's eyes and gave him only the truth. 'He has nothing now. He is an empty gourd; soon he will dry and break into shards. He used what he had: a fast gun and an unfeeling heart. He is a killer with no man to name him friend or brother.'

The old man's face began to fade, to recede back into the red mist, and his voice was only a thread of sound when he said, 'Trust the truth of your dreams. Trust.' And then he was gone, taking the sunshine with him, leaving Rogue adrift in a cold and barren land where neither pain nor dreams could exist.

★　★　★

Light returned, brought with it heat, his own burning. Motion stopped. Voices laughed, cried. Hands pulled at him, hurt him, carried him, left him on something soft.

Rogue opened his eyes, saw a face.

'Leave me be!' He tried to shout the words as the face came nearer, the face that had haunted his dreams for as long as he could remember. But he had enough sense left to know that this wasn't the same dream. This face was real. It came closer, wavered to his seeing, and grew. It was too much to bear. Rogue closed his eyes.

'Is he dead?' Rogue heard a soft, weary-sounding voice ask, a woman's voice.

It was Haskins' voice that answered. 'No, missus, not yet. He was a-jabbering and a-carrying on in some kind of Injun talk a ways back, and then he started a-shaking something fierce, like he was freezing. Now, he don't know a blamed thing. I reckon he's a goner for sure.'

Shorty added, 'Ma'am, I dug out the lead and burned over the wounds, but they broke open on the way down the mountain. He's a-bleeding bad. I'd say he ain't got a chance of making it, and, ma'am, that makes me hurt a mite. By my reckoning, he's a good man.'

Rogue opened his eyes, tried to peer into the gloom that filled the room — or wherever he was. She was still there. Deidre, the woman with black hair, was older now, and she wasn't weeping, but she was still the same.

She reached out, put her cool hand on his forehead. Trying to pull away from that gentle touch, Rogue wanted to scream, 'No, don't touch me,' but weakness had stolen his voice.

'Love,' she asked, 'who is he? My darling Patrick would have looked just so if God had but granted him the extra years.'

'Please, my dear, don't,' Faith's father said, sounding soft, loving, and tired. 'Your boy is dead, you know that. Do not think this man is your son. He is no one you would want to claim as kin. Ben is sure this is Lejube Rogue, you know, the gunfighter folks talk about? I don't know for sure who he is, but I don't . . . He saved both our kids, I couldn't just go off and let him die — even if I do know that trouble follows his kind. I wish . . . '

Deidre stopped him. 'Love, if the devil saved my wee ones, I would bid him welcome in my house.'

'Yes, my dear, I know. Care for him. We owe him that and more, but I beg you, do not overdo. Your health is always my first concern.'

'I will have Daisy do the tending, but I can only give this young man honor. He saved my children and . . . Love, I could not survive the loss of another child. I have lost too much. First, my Patrick and then my babies. Too much.'

Rogue only sighed, but somewhere within him a small boy cried bitterly, cried for the mother who didn't know him. And he welcomed the darkness when it came. It took him away from the sad-faced woman, and he was glad. He didn't have the strength to look upon that face, the face of the mother who had deserted him, left him to the tender mercies of his merciless grandfather.

And he most certainly didn't have the strength to face this new truth. His mother had run away with the man who had gunned down his father. Dolph Odom. The man Rogue had sworn to kill. And if she was here, then he was here also.

But wherever they were, whatever they had done, he couldn't come close to keeping the vow he had sworn to a dying man. Lejube Rogue didn't have enough strength left to lift one of his Colts, let alone aim and fire it. He ran from the thought, surrendered to the weakness, and went, a willing prisoner, with the darkness.

11

He knew time was passing, but Rogue could only twist with pain, burn with fever, and pull himself partially out of his stupor when someone tended him. He swallowed the liquids that someone held to his cracked lips. He knew momentary relief when someone bathed him with cool water. He dreamed, dreamed always, of Eagle Flying, of his mother, and of — other things, nightmare things born in his childhood. And perhaps he spoke aloud; he didn't truly know.

Once or twice he thought he heard the sounds of guns, of women screaming. Again and again he tried to get up, shouted for his Colts, knew, even in the depths of his dreaming, Faith was in danger.

Hands pushed him down, held him. Soft voices spoke soothing words until he was calm. Faith sat beside his bed and talked and talked — he listened to her voice, but he didn't know what she said.

Just how much time had passed, Rogue couldn't say for sure, but finally he opened his eyes and knew he would live. Moving a little, he felt only a slight twinge of pain. The fever haze was gone; he saw things clearly.

Rogue knew he was in a bed, a real bed with cool white sheets and fluffy feather pillows. The bed was in the corner of a big room built of logs that had been adzed square and chinked tight with clay and moss. It was clean and uncluttered, but it looked like people lived there.

A small fire flickered in the smoke-blackened fireplace, and a coal oil lamp cast a warm glow on a table near the stone fireplace. A plump woman sat on a bench close by the table. Knitting needles flashed in her hands, and the firelight behind her turned her mass of untidy, blondish-gray hair into a halo.

Rogue knew the woman, whoever she was, wasn't Deidre, but he didn't know if Deidre had really been here or whether that, too, had been a part of his fevered dreaming.

'Who?' he asked, and weakness had turned his voice into a harsh, rasping whisper.

She jumped. The ball of yarn fell from her lap, unrolled across the puncheon floor. 'Oooooooohhhh! Mister, you like to scared me into a conniption. I thought you was still dead to the world. What with all the burning and shooting that's been going on around here, I'm as edgy as a broody hen.'

'Shooting?'

'Land a-Goshen, mister, I did it again. Forget what I said. The missus will fair skin me alive if she finds out what I said. You ain't supposed to be worrying none until you're well. Oh, good grief, when will I ever learn to keep my big mouth shut?'

It wasn't a question that needed

165

answering, but Rogue had some that did. 'The outlaws? They came here?'

'I ain't saying a-nother word. You just lay there and rest easy. I'll go fetch the missus.' She got to her feet, huffing a little with the effort, mumbling under her breath. She paused just long enough to give Rogue a quick look before she turned and almost ran through the doorway in the wall opposite the bed.

Rogue took a deep breath and didn't even wonder at the lack of pain. He barely noticed; his thoughts were too intent on other, and far older, pain. It might have been a dream, but if it wasn't, he wasn't ready to face the woman he thought was his mother. Within seconds, he could hear the woman's high-pitched voice in the next room, but he couldn't understand a word she was saying.

He had no time to brood or even prepare himself for a meeting too long delayed. Deidre came slowly into the room, trailed by the plump woman and

Faith. Her eyes were set in tear-puffed flesh, and their blueness had faded to almost gray. She smiled a watery smile at Rogue.

He saw she was older, much older, than she had been when the miniature he still carried in his medicine pouch was painted. His hand reached up, touched the little leather pouch that hung around his neck, and he almost sighed. Once it had had great meaning, but now it held only the picture, the picture of a young and very beautiful woman.

Rogue took another deep breath and steeled himself against the concern he could see on this unknown person's soft, wrinkled face. 'Did the outlaws come?' he asked, his voice colder and harsher than he wanted it to be, but he had no other choice. This woman, the woman who had given him life, was married to the man he had sworn to kill. He would not let a small, lonely boy's memory of love sway him from that promise. Lejube Rogue would kill

Dolph Odom, Deidre's husband, just as the man had killed Rogue's father.

'Sure and I'm glad to see you with us again, lad,' she said. 'You have been fevered and raving for a time and a time, but now you have a healing look.'

She turned away from him to the others. 'Faith, fetch some water in the basin. The young man will feel all the better after a good wash. Daisy, the chicken broth is on the hearth there. Push it closer to the fire and give it a bit of heating. He needs to eat — look how gaunt he is, poor lad,' she said, and her voice was tired and old — there was nothing left of the warm, lilting joy that spoke in Rogue's memory.

Trying to drive away yesterday's bits and pieces, Rogue shook his head. He couldn't come close to keeping his vow to his grandfather, the promise to Faith had to come first.

If what Daisy had said was true, he had to have some answers and quickly. He edged over in the bed, slid his feet from under the covers, and tried to rise.

'My clothes?' he asked.

'Oh, no you don't, lad. Have some sense. You've been lost to all knowing for more than four days. You aren't going anywhere until you have a little more time to mend.' Deidre applied gentle pressure to his shoulders, and he sank back onto the bed, feeling a little grateful. He wasn't ready to do any traveling yet, not unless he wanted to fall flat on his face.

She brushed back Rogue's hair and put her hand on his forehead. 'Well, lad, 'tis sure and certain that you're a strong one. There's no fire left in you, and when I changed your bandages earlier, your great wounds were already scabbing and healing. If you eat well and rest this day, I will allow you to test your legs on the morrow.'

He listened with scant attention and voiced his real worry when he asked, 'The outlaws?'

'Let that be someone's else's trouble. Just you rest and . . . '

He looked her full in the face, and

there wasn't any softness in him when he demanded, 'Did they come here? The outlaws? Is that who was doing all the shooting?'

Her face fell into lines of sadness, and her white fingers plucked at the quilt that covered Rogue. 'Yes, lad,' she finally whispered, 'they came.'

Rogue waited for her to continue.

Her chin quivered like a hurt child's, but she tried to straighten her slumped shoulders as she firmed her lips, took a deep breath, and said, 'My dear husband said, and not without truth, that this new trouble is none of yours. Already you have done more than enough for me and mine. Not ever will I forget you. Every day that I live, I will give thanks and ask the Good Lord to keep you from all harm.'

Swallowing, trying to smile, she said, 'I can do naught else, but I can pray for you. Those two, Robby and Faith, are all the children God spared me. The others . . . '

'Mama,' Faith said, watching her

mother closely as she walked across the room to the bedside, 'here's Mr. Rogue's bath water. Why don't you take Daisy and go out to the summer kitchen. There's . . . '

'Faith, love, don't look at me so. I'm not going to be sick again. It's just that . . . It's so senseless, so cruel. Why did those men tear up my babies' graves? Why? My poor, wee babes harmed no one. They were scarce upon this earth before the Lord called them home. Why did . . . '

'Mama, Daisy's going to need . . . I just looked at the bread dough. It needs to be worked down before it runs over the top of the crock and . . . '

'Dear heavens, the bread! I'll take care of it at once. Faith, I don't know what's wrong with me. I seem to forget even the simplest things.' She turned, started away, and stopped at the doorway to ask, 'If Daisy goes with me, do you know what needs doing in here?'

'Yes, Mama. I'll take care of Mr. Rogue.'

'Daisy had best . . . Rogue? Who is . . . oh, yes. But, it's a horrible name, and it just . . . ' Deidre murmured as she left the room alone, leaving Daisy still poking at the fire in the fireplace, pushing an iron pot into the bed of coals.

Not entirely ignoring the presence of the plump woman, Rogue pitched his voice low when he said, 'Tell me about the outlaws.'

Faith didn't hesitate. 'They came twice, a whole bunch of them. I guess Papa has to believe us now.'

'I suppose, but . . . Was anyone hurt?'

'Not by the shooting,' she said softly, her voice shaking like she was just about ready to cry.

'Don't let it get you,' Rogue said. 'Tell me what happened, maybe we can figure out something from that.'

'Mr. Rogue, Mama doesn't want you bothered, but I have to talk to somebody. Papa, Robby, and the men are worried, but they just . . . I don't think they know what to do. The outlaws are . . . You know.'

'Start at the beginning,' he said, and he heard the growl of anger in his own voice, knew he had frightened her, but didn't know how to make it right.

Her eyes big, she backed away from the bed, sloshing water over the rim of the tin basin she still held. 'I'd better go see about Mama. Daisy can . . . '

'Faith,' Rogue said, 'do what you have to do, but don't ever run scared. I'm not going to hurt you. I would never hurt you — you must know that.'

Her hands still shook, and so did her voice when she said, 'Y-y-y-yes, I know, but, Mr. Rogue, Mama has been so bad, and Ben keeps saying mean things about . . . I don't like him one little bit, but he keeps talking and Papa keeps listening and . . . '

Daisy rose from the hearth, put her hands on her ample hips, and began to give Faith the sharp side of her tongue. 'Look what you're doing, spilling water all over my clean floor. Ain't we got enough trouble without you . . . You're gonna drive your mother to an early grave; the woman's a saint, and the way you kids act is a crime. Running off to the mountains and getting mixed up with a killer like . . . ' She glared at Rogue and the girl alike, turned, and left the room, still grumbling something about ungrateful kids and women's sorry lot in life.

'She's just talking mostly,' Faith said. 'She thinks Mama is wonderful, but I don't think she cares much about anything else.'

Sighing just a little, she tried to smile at him as she hooked her toe around a chair leg and pulled it over next to the bed. She sat the basin of water on the chair's caned seat and leaned against the side of the bed, looking down at him. She stood silent for a moment or two before she said, 'What those outlaws are doing, just doesn't make any sense. We don't know who they are, or why they're doing such terrible things.'

Rogue started to ask, 'Like what?' but

she continued before he could get the words out. 'Back there, where you hid Robby, they shot only one time. You fell off your horse and . . . They didn't shoot anymore or anything. They just stayed out in the dark, where we couldn't see them, and they laughed. It sounded like they were all around us, and maybe they were, I don't know.'

She swallowed, swallowed again, and went on, 'One of them shouted, 'That's just to show you what we can do, Odom, but don't be a-worrying none. You'll get to see everything, 'cause we're gonna save you for dead last. First, we're gonna burn your house, burn your barn, kill your cattle, your men, and that boy of yourn.' '

Clamping her teeth together to stop them from chattering, Faith reached out, put her trembling hand on top of his, and whispered, 'I was so . . . I thought you were dead and I . . . Mr. Rogue, you won't let them do what . . . They said they were going to hurt Mama and me, real bad, and do it right

175

in front of Papa, and then they rode away, laughing like they were all crazy.'

He put his other hand on top of her small one and repeated the promise he had made back in the canyon. 'I will never allow them to touch you again.'

'Thank you,' she whispered before she withdrew her hand, squared her skinny little shoulders and said, 'Papa is Odom, Dolph Odom.'

It wasn't a truth he wanted to contemplate; not at that moment. His time would come with Odom later, but his promise to Faith had to come first, and he had to know as much as possible about the outlaws before he could figure out how to keep it. 'I know who your father is,' he said. 'Go on. Tell me what happened next. What happened here.'

'Nothing much happened. You had passed out, so they loaded you on the horse, and we came home as quickly as we could. Then, about three nights ago, well, really early in the morning, they sneaked in and set fire to the bunkhouse. Then they started yelling and shooting. They laughed and shouted bad things and shot at the house for about an hour, and then, when it wasn't hardly light, they rode off, still laughing.

'We put out the fire. Nothing much was hurt, except . . . When it was full light, I found Toby. He was Shorty's dog, and he was old and almost blind, but . . . He was such a good dog that . . . I cried, and I think Shorty did, too. Papa doesn't like dogs, but I played with Toby every day and . . . Those men shot him and left him to bleed to death. They shot that poor old dog and . . . '

'I'm sorry, kid,' Rogue said softly. Her choked cry of grief had made him feel something he hadn't felt in a long time, but he couldn't allow his growing affection for the girl, his half-sister, change the vow he had given his grandfather. Could he? It was a question he didn't want to ponder, especially not now.

'I'm all right, Mr. Rogue, really I am. It's just that we don't know what those men are going to do next, and we haven't had much sleep.'

Rogue hated to keep her talking about things that were hurting her so, but there was no one else to ask, and he had to know. 'Why was your mother crying?'

12

Faith stood there, biting her lower lip, twisting her hands together until Rogue asked again, 'Why was your mother crying?'

'The outlaws . . . ' she gulped, swallowed, and went on, 'came again this morning. This time they waited until it was light enough for us to see what they were doing.'

Rogue thought she had said all she could, but she surprised him by lifting her chin and going on. 'There's a little graveyard out by where the meadow and the trees come together. Mama lost three little babies and a bigger boy, my brother, Patrick, before Robby and I were born. They're buried there. Papa built a fence around it and painted it white. This morning the outlaws tied ropes onto the fence and tore it down. Then they rode their horses back and forth across those little graves, tromping all the flowers Mama had planted, tearing up the grave markers Shorty had carved.

'It was awful, Mr. Rogue, Papa couldn't do anything to stop the ones who were in the graveyard. The rest of the bunch was shooting at the house. We just had to stay in here and listen to Mama cry.'

The sadness in her soft little voice reached right into Rogue's heart, but he didn't dare show it. Nor did he dare wonder how the boy he had been, how Patrick Scanlon had got to be buried in a grave in Oregon, in a place he had never been. If that question needed asking, there would be time enough later, but for now, all he could do was listen to Faith's recitation of horror and nurse his own hurt in silence.

'When they got tired of tearing up the graves, the outlaws piled up the fence and the wooden markers and set them on fire. Then the whole gang of them rode off and . . . and they were still laughing.

'Why would they do that to the graves? It hurt Mama bad, made her almost sick again. She was out at graveyard at least once every day, carrying water for the flowers, whispering things to her little boy and the babies. I don't know what she told them, but I think she kept saying she was sorry. Once, when she was real sick and kind of crying, I heard her tell Papa that she thought God took her children because he was punishing her for something she did a long time ago.'

Rogue couldn't help asking, 'What?'

'I don't know, maybe nothing. She's really sweet. I don't think she could have done very much that was bad; she's too good.' She edged up onto the side of the bed and sat down.

After the quiet had stretched a long way, she opened her mouth, looked at Rogue, looked down, and finally said, the words coming out in a tangled rush, 'Mr. Rogue, will you help us? Papa said

181

not to ask, he said we couldn't afford to hire your gun but I'm so afraid and you're the only one who . . . Please, say you'll help us. We don't have anybody else.' She covered her thin, freckled face with her hands, and the bed shook with the force of her sobs.

Thoughts warring with each other, conflicting promises tearing at him, Rogue looked at his sister, Dolph Odom's daughter, and knew that he would never break the promise he had made to her. Patrick Scanlon might be dead and buried, but Lejube Rogue would stand in his stead, would stay and kill his sister's tormentors. And then? He had no answer. He didn't know if he could keep the promise he had made to his grandfather. He didn't know whether he could ever cause this little girl that much grief — but his word was his bond, something he had always kept.

'Stop crying,' he said, trying to keep his voice soft, 'and tell me what your father meant about not having enough money to hire my gun. I don't fight for money.'

Her shoulders still shook.

'Listen, Faith, didn't I make you a promise in the canyon and make it again when we were out there in that pile of rocks? Don't you know Lejube Rogue always keeps his word?'

Her head came up, and she stared at him for a moment before she reached over and tried to hug him. He held her away. She smiled at him and said, 'I knew you would help. I told Mama that you would never just ride away and leave me here to be hurt. And, Mr. Rogue, no matter what the rest of them did, I didn't listen to Ben, I didn't believe one word he said.'

'Thanks,' he said before adding, 'I'm tired now, why don't you run and talk to your mama while I take a little nap?' He closed his eyes after he spoke, but it wasn't weariness that made him send her away. Too much had happened too soon, and he needed time to think, to try to understand what she had told him. The future loomed dark before him, and he knew, one way or another, he was going to hurt her, hurt her real bad.

* * *

'Nobody ever thanked a damned fool 'cept with a bullet. Do you hear me, boy?' His grandfather's words seemed to run around inside Rogue's head. They were so plain that he almost expected to feel the bull whip slash across his back to add meaning to the words.

'A man's got to do what he thinks is right, no matter who gets hurt in the doing,' Rogue muttered as he turned and twisted in the bed, making it creak and rustle in time with his tortured thoughts.

After sending Faith away, he had thought long and hard about the situation he had gotten himself into and hadn't gotten anywhere close to finding a solution to the problem when he had fallen into a fitful sleep.

184

The promise he had made to Faith wasn't a problem. The outlaws deserved to die for what they had done to Robby and her, and he would have no more thought about destroying them than he would about any other rabid skunk.

It was the other promise that plagued his thoughts. It seemed like, if he was a man of his word, that he had to keep that promise, too. He made no claims to being good — he'd killed too many men to lay claim to that — but he had never broken his given word. If he gunned down the outlaws and rode away without killing the man who had murdered his own father what would that make him? A liar? A man without honor? A faithless man? Could such a man return to Eagle Flying, or would the loss of honor take away whatever power he had left?

But if he did kill Dolph Odom, what then? Could he live out his life knowing he had caused that little girl so much pain? It wasn't a question he could come close to answering.

Rogue slept, and in his dreams, Eagle Flying looked at him, watched him with white, sightless eyes. It was as if he were teaching something Rogue couldn't or wouldn't understand. Rogue bowed his head. His growing unease woke him before he could beg wisdom and understanding from the old shaman.

Feeling too confused, too prickly, to sleep again, Rogue hitched himself up in the bed, leaned against the wall, and examined the bed. It was just a pole frame fastened to the wall with wooden pegs and laced with leather strips. The mattress ticking was stuffed with sweet-smelling meadow grass, and the sheets were muslin that had been washed and sun-bleached to a soft white. A hand-pieced quilt was spread over the top.

The need to be up and moving tugged at him. Easing his feet over the edge of the bed, moving slow and careful, he sat up and waited for the dizziness to come swooping in. It didn't come. He was weak, stiff, and hurting just a little; his stomach growled with hunger; but he could sit without toppling over — and that was a step in the right direction.

His fever was gone, but the room was hot, with the only real light coming from a single, smoke-blacked lamp. The shutters on the four, small windows were closed and barred. A few streaks of sunlight leaked through the cracks, but no breeze entered to relieve the room's stuffy, almost smothering heat.

Sweat soaked his body and made him aware of his burning thirst. He stood and started to take a cautious step toward a water bucket he could see across the room.

Voices muffled by the thick slabs of wood sounded outside the door at the foot of the bed. Rogue glanced in that direction just as he realized he was naked, except for the tight bandages around his chest, shoulder, and thigh. He sat down, pulled the quilt around him, and waited, muscles tense, wishing for his Colts, for whoever was outside to come in.

He let out a breath he didn't know he was holding when the door opened in, and Shorty and Haskins, battered hats in their hands, came tiptoeing in grinning a little and trying not to look sheepish.

'Howdy, Rogue,' Haskins said, his voice not much more than a whisper.

Unsure what was going on, Rogue nodded a greeting to both men and waited.

'We ain't supposed to be in here. The boss gave orders that you was to be left plumb alone. But we figgered we could sneak in and have us a quick visit without nobody a-being the wiser,' Shorty said, his voice not much louder than Haskins's had been.

Gripping the brim of his hat with both hands, Haskins cleared his throat, looked at Shorty, cleared his throat again. Finally, speaking in halts and stops, he said, 'Uh, Rogue, maybe we're a-speaking outta turn, but we, me and

Shorty here, we think . . . Well, sir, something gotta be done and . . . Uh, you see, the boss and Ben've been a-doing a heap of private talking, but . . . Rogue, I tell you true, we dunno what to think. They ain't really been doing nothing, and . . . '

Shorty broke in with, 'The missus was hurt real bad by what them devils did to her babies' graves. I know Miss Faith is like to be a-jumping outta her hide. Daisy ain't no better — she's been a-burning food or a-forgetting to cook it. Me and Haskins, we don't think it's right to be a-sitting around twiddling our thumbs while the womenfolk are in danger.'

Haskins nodded his head in agreement, and both men watched Rogue like they expected something from him. Not knowing for sure where the talk was heading, even if he did have an inkling or two, Rogue waited without speaking.

The punchers looked at each other, shuffled their feet, tugged at their hats, cleared their throats. The silence got longer and longer, until Shorty broke it.

'Rogue, this is a mite hard for us to be a-saying. We . . . uh . . . Meaning no offense, but . . . this is the first time we . . . We know you're a whole lot tougher than . . . Likely you'll be up and a-doing in a day or two. When that happens, the boss is a-figgering on giving you a horse so's you can ride out of here.' He stopped, looked at Haskins, and started gnawing on his bottom lip.

'I already have a horse, two in fact,' Rogue said. 'I have no need for anything Dolph Odom wants to give me. And I'll ride when I'm good and ready.'

Shorty sort of flicked a glance in Rogue's direction and then looked down at the floor. 'I'm right sorry, son, I reckon that came out wrong. I've been with the boss for a long time, his family owned me once, and generally speaking, he's a right smart man. It's only in the last while that he's been a-listening and a-taking for Gospel everything Ben

190

says. It's passing strange, but I reckon, sooner or later, he'll come to his senses — iffen it ain't too late.'

Haskins licked his lips before he said, 'Well, sir, what we come in here for was to . . . It's like this. Well, you see, me and Shorty, we saved up a little dab of money and . . . Now, it ain't much, but we . . . '

'Don't say it,' Rogue said, cringing a little at the coldness in his own voice but not backing off. 'I promised Faith that those men would never hurt her again. Do you think I'm going to break my word?'

'No, sir, we didn't,' Shorty answered, but he flinched away from whatever he thought he saw in Rogue's narrowed eyes.

'Son,' Haskins said, 'we told you once we trusted you, and we meant it. It's just that it don't seem right for a man to maybe die just to keep a promise. We wanted to give you . . . '

Rogue asked, 'If a man must die for something, is it better to die for money?'

191

'No, it ain't. It ain't better to die for anything, but we ... I reckon we're a-playing the fool, but we didn't mean to hurt you none, and that's for damned true.'

'I'm not hurt or angry,' Rogue said, 'but I don't fight for hire either.'

'I reckon we know that now, son, but iffen you won't take our money, can you take my hand?' Shorty asked, extending his hand.

'I'm proud to shake your hand,' Rogue said, meaning every word.

Grinning widely, Haskins said, 'Can I get you something? It 'pears like the womenfolk have been a-neglecting you something fierce.'

Responding to the men's proffered friendship, Rogue tried to smile. 'I'm thirsty,' he said, 'and from the way my stomach's behaving, I think I could eat a cow or two.'

'Well, sir, I can go out to the spring and get you the best and the coldest drinking water in these here parts, but I dunno about a-getting you any grub.

That there Daisy now, well, she's a holy terror in the kitchen. If I went in there, a-poking around, she might just about do anything, but most probable she'd grab that big iron skillet and . . . Rogue, you'd purely hate to see a full-growed man cry, wouldn't you? Why I recollect this one time, it must've been a-closing on to six-months gone that I . . . '

Even if he had wanted to, Rogue couldn't have held back the chuckle that rose in his throat. 'Haskins,' he said, 'if you don't get me that water, I'm not going to live long enough to hear the rest of your story.'

Grinning, Haskins tugged on his hat, walked across, grabbed the water bucket, and headed for the door. It opened before he could do much more than reach for it. Skinny as his sister, awkward, and scared-looking, Robby slipped into the room without saying a word — and Rogue's gunbelts and holstered Colts were dangling from his hand.

'Robby, you'd better be a-hustling

yourself outta here. You heard what your pa said. He'll purely skin you iffen he catches you in here a-talking to Rogue,' Haskins said as he passed the boy and went out.

Ignoring the warning, the boy walked over to the bed and said, 'I didn't come to bother you, sir, but I had to come and give you my thanks. I don't know how you healed me up so quick, but even if Papa and Ben do think it was only a scratch, I know how bad I was hit. And I know I'd be dead now instead of just having a scar if you hadn't come along when you did. I appreciate what you did for me and . . . Thank you.'

Rogue tried to smile, but the bleakness within him kept it at bay. The boy's face was too much like his own — but it was so terribly young. Just looking at him gave Rogue a flicker of some kind of emotion. Robby was his brother and even if he couldn't claim the kinship, it was still there. He would be hurting his own brother if he killed

Dolph Odom, but . . . He sucked in a breath of air and pushed the turmoil out of the front of his thoughts.

'Sir, I brought your guns. I thought you might need . . . Ben said he was going to . . . I thought you'd like it better if they were close to hand.'

'I appreciate it,' Rogue said, letting his hand fall across the weapons when the boy placed them carefully in Rogue's lap.

'I cleaned and oiled them. They're loaded. I just wanted to do . . . I was really careful, but Papa says I can't do anything right, so maybe you ought to look them over and . . . '

'No need. I trust you.'

'Faith helped. She said . . . Are you really going to stay here and . . . '

Rogue nodded.

'I'm glad. We really need . . . '

'We really need what?' a harsh voice asked as Ben walked in through the opposite door with Dolph Odom close behind. 'Speak up, you sneaking whelp, what do we need this dirty killer for?'

13

Ben swaggered into the room like he owned it and several more just like it. He hadn't a glance to spare for Shorty, but he gave Rogue a narrow look before he took Robby's arm, gave it a shake, and said, 'What's the matter, boy? The cat got your tongue? Or is your big talk sticking in your craw now that you've been caught?'

Odom took a hand. 'Easy, Ben,' he said, stepping around his foreman to face his son. 'Robby, I told you to stay away from here. You have work to finish, so get to it. Your mother needs some firewood split and carried in. I don't want to have to tell you twice. Now get out of here and stay out.'

After a quick look at the Colts on Rogue's lap, Robby smiled, a sort of a secret, closed-in smile like he knew something the rest of the world didn't, and walked out without saying another thing. He was obeying his father, but his back was straight and there was nothing hangdog about him.

The door was still closing behind Robby when Ben frowned at Rogue. He looked riled and meaner than seemed real proper given all the givens. 'Now, Boss, are you gonna tell this snake what we decided, or do you want me to make sure he knows he ain't wanted around these parts?'

'Thanks for offering, Ben, but there are some things a man has to do for himself,' Odom answered. He took a seat on the end of the bed and sat staring at Rogue like there was something about him that needed knowing. 'You look . . . ' He shook his head before he went on, saying, 'I'm beholden to you for saving my kids, and I know there's no way I can make up to you for what happened, but . . . '

Odom looked at Rogue like he was trying to see through the gloom or searching his memory, and again he gave his head a shake, but the puzzled look stayed on his face. He went on, his words not quite hanging together, but sort of jumping from place to place. 'I want you to stay here until you're healed and ready to ride. I'll give you a horse, replenish your supplies, and throw in a little gold. That should square things up a little.'

He should have felt something, hate maybe, or anger, or even a little sadness, but Rogue looked at his father's killer and felt nothing — not even the certainty that he would someday kill this man to keep a vow made to a dying man. He wanted to sigh, but it was neither the time nor the place, so he sat there, returning Odom's stare, and waited.

'Ben says you charge high, and I can't afford to hire you, but that isn't why I want you to leave. No matter who you are, you have to know that no decent man would want his kids to be mixed up with your kind.'

'Just what is my kind, Mr. Odom?'

Rogue asked softly, surprised he really wanted an answer, wanted to hear what this man, the man who had murdered Rogue's father and stolen his mother, would have to say.

It wasn't Odom who answered. 'You're a murdering, lying bastard, and ain't nobody safe while you're around,' Ben snarled.

Ben was trying, real hard, to appear angry, but beneath the talk there was something else, something cold and calculating. Ben's words had been chosen to provoke Rogue into a fight, and Rogue wondered why. It had to be more than just a chance to win a little fame by gunning down Lejube Rogue, but what?

Nothing would be gained by answering Ben's insults, so Rogue just watched Ben's eyes, smiled, and let his fingers caress the butt of one of the Colts Robby had returned to him — fully-loaded Colts that had killed before and probably would again — but he wasn't above doing a little game-playing of his own.

Ben wasn't a patient man. 'Say something, you lying, no account,' he almost screamed as his hand went down to hover over the handle of the gun hanging low on his hip.

Keeping his smile in place and his voice easy, Rogue said, 'Ben, I've heard that fear can be a troubling thing, but you shouldn't let it bother you like this. If a man isn't used to being shot at, I reckon what's been going on around here might upset him a little.

'There's no need to take it out on me, is there? If you're spoiling for fight, you'd better look someplace else. I don't shoot little boys with big ideas.' Rogue let his smile get wider but not a bit warmer than winter ice.

Ben sputtered, 'Damn you, I'm as old as you are, maybe older. I ain't no damned coward,' and went for his gun.

Shorty lunged, grabbed Ben's arm, and hung on tight. 'What in blazes is wrong with you, Ben?' he shouted. 'How's it gonna help us to have Rogue kill you?'

'Ben,' Odom thundered, 'stop acting the fool. Put that gun away at once. You know what shooting does to my wife, are you . . . Put it away!'

Ben muttered an oath, but after a slight hesitation, he obeyed. He glared at Rogue before he looked at Odom and said, 'I'm sorry, Boss, you know I wouldn't do nothing to hurt the missus. I didn't mean to . . . Dammit, just looking at him makes me so mad I . . .'

He took a deep breath and went on. 'Boss, I know he's mixed up with them outlaws. He has to be! Why else would a big-time hired gun like him be a-nosing around down in these parts? Hell, there ain't been a speck of trouble here since you strung up them Butlers. If he ain't in with that gang, why is he here? Ask him, Boss. Just ask him.'

Looking real thoughtful, Odom pushed his fingers through his thick hair and sat a moment longer before he said, 'Son, Ben has a point. Just why are you down here?'

'Mr. Odom,' Rogue said, making no

effort to keep the flat coldness out of his voice, 'that is none of your business.' And he meant it.

Only one man, Eagle Flying, could understand the need that brought Rogue to Southern Oregon — and it wasn't the vague rumors he had heard about Odom's whereabouts. When he left the Columbia River at The Dalles and traveled down the length of Oregon, he was searching for something else.

Once the old shaman had told the boy of a deep-blue lake set high in the Cascades. The white men had named it Crater Lake and taken it as their own, but they had not been able to steal its medicine.

The old gods had battled there and blew the top off of a mighty mountain. Now it was a place of peace, dreams, and seeing, but it had held nothing for Rogue. Five days he had spent there, fasting and seeking, and then he had rode away as empty as he had come.

He had thought then that the lake

could grant him nothing until he had kept the vow, killed the man who had murdered his father. Now, he knew that wasn't true; the killing would only make him emptier still. There would never be any peace for the man folks called Lejube Rogue.

'See, Boss, what did I tell you? He ain't got no answer 'cause he's in with them outlaws,' Ben said, sounding far too eager, even if Rogue couldn't even guess the why of it.

And maybe Shorty was having a few doubts also. 'Boss,' he said, 'if you listen to Ben here, you might be a-jumping the gun. Rogue ain't no hired killer; he never was. And he ain't the sort of man who'd run with a pack of dog killers. It 'pears to me you're a-being a mite harsh on a man who ain't done a thing except save your young'uns. The way I see it, you're a-poking in something that ain't your look-in, and you're insulting a man who purely don't deserve it.'

Odom shifted on the bed, turned

slightly to look at Shorty. He sounded almost sad when he said, 'We've been together since we were boys. I never thought you'd turn on me like this.'

'We've been together right enough, but first I was a slave and now your hired hand. That might make us friends, but it don't mean I can't speak what's on my mind. The way I see it, Rogue here is a stranger, but he ain't done you nothing but good.

'I kinda hate to say this again, but I reckon it needs repeating. The way I see it, you'd be a heap better off if you did your own thinking instead of a-letting a nobody like Ben here tell you what to do.'

Rogue kept his eyes on Ben, and he wasn't surprised when the foreman turned red, took two steps toward the puncher, and started shouting. 'You doddering old fool! What right have you got to be a-talking about me like that? I'm a better man than you've ever been, and the boss is smart enough to know it. Now you'd better shut that flapping mouth of yours, old man, if you don't want a bullet in your gut. Hell, I've shot tougher men than you for a hell of lot less.'

His hat still in his hands, Shorty stood his ground.

'Yeah, Ben,' he said, talking quiet and slow, 'I reckon we all heard how brave you are. I figger it takes a whole mess of courage to walk up to a Chinaman and shoot him dead the way you did in Jacksonville last year. Yessir, a mess of courage — the way I heard it, the old man didn't even have a gun.'

Ben's voice got quieter, too, and maybe it sounded a little sullen. 'Why're you a-bringing that up now. That didn't take any courage, he was only a Chink. Hell, me and the boys was just a-having a mite of fun — the judge only fined me for shooting inside the city limits. I don't know what that has to do with nothing.'

'He was a man,' Shorty said, 'and you shot him down like he was less than dirt.'

'Naw, he wasn't. He was just a Chink. And, why in the hell are you jawing about it now?'

'Forget it, Ben,' Shorty said, giving a kind sigh. 'I just wanted the boss to see what kind of man he was trusting.'

'Shorty, I figger you're talking bad about me, but I don't . . . Hell, if you've got something a-sticking in your black gizzard, why don't you come right out and say it. I ain't gonna take no bad-mouthing from a dirty nig . . . '

'That's enough from both of you,' Odom snapped. He stood up, looked down at Rogue, and said bluntly, 'I don't want you here any longer than necessary. As soon as you can ride, I want you gone. Regardless of what Shorty and the kids think of you, I don't see much to admire in a killer.'

'Neither do I, Odom,' Rogue said. 'But, no matter what you say, I am not going to ride off and leave Faith at the mercy of those men. Besides, you need every gun you can get, and you know it.'

'I don't want you here, and I don't need you. Ben is riding out tonight, going down to the valley to hire some men and bring them back. That will take care of any problem we might have.'

Shorty wasn't convinced. 'Yeah, but how long'll that take? Three, maybe four days? You don't know, maybe he'll have to ride all the way to Jacksonville to find enough men. How are we gonna hold out until then?'

'We'll just fort up here. I built this house to hold off Indians. I doubt a few outlaws can break in.'

'Boss, you know dang well there's more than a few.'

'God, Shorty,' Ben said, 'ain't you got enough sense to let it lay? The boss has already said what's what, so either shut-up or draw your time; that way we'd be rid of you and your pet killer both.'

Rogue's hand never left the Colts in his lap. He couldn't tell for sure which way Odom was going to jump or what

Ben was trying to pull. He was grateful when Haskins returned with a full bucket of water. It broke the tension and gave everyone a little time to cool-off, but before anything was actually settled, Daisy came stomping in and sent the whole bunch of them scooting.

'You, Haskins,' she said, 'give the boy a drink, and the rest of you get yourselves outta here right now. This boy is supposed to be a-getting some rest. Look at the lot of you, standing around, talking loud, when there's work a-plenty that needs doing. Men do beat all. Out! Out!' Daisy said, and she flapped her apron at them like she was shooing chickens. 'You, too, Mr. Odom. The missus needs you. The poor soul's been a-crying again.'

The men left in a hurry and without a word. Rogue understood why when she rounded on him and demanded, 'What are you doing sitting up? Didn't the missus tell you to stay in that bed?'

'I was hungry and thirsty, and I . . . '

'Applesauce! You young varmint, you got up 'cause you're as wrong-headed as any mule in the country, and you know it,' she snapped. 'Now, drink some of that water Haskins fetched and get back in the bed. I ain't a-hankering to feed no jaybird-nakid man.'

Haskins had left the water bucket beside the bed and Rogue wasn't slow in drinking his fill of the icy water. The plump woman returned the bucket to its original spot, picked up the basin Faith had left earlier, and stood a minute studying him before she said, 'Bed,' and left the room.

Rogue barely had time to get in bed, pushing the pillows up so he could make a backrest and lean against the wall, tucking the Colts beneath a fold of the quilt, when Shorty stuck his head through the door outside. He said, 'See you later, Rogue. The boss figgers we'll all be safer if Haskins and me move into the house while Ben's gone.' He gave Rogue a grin and a whispered, 'Gotta go. Daisy's a-coming.'

Puffing and wheezing, Daisy walked in carrying a goodly amount of food on a tray. She sat it down on a chair beside the bed and stood there. 'I don't grudge no man his vittles, boy, but I want you outta here and real soon.'

Weariness taking his appetite, Rogue licked his lips before he asked, 'Why?'

'You did a heap of talking when you was off your head. I didn't rightly understand most of what you was jabbering, but I know you're up to no good. I'll tell you this, and you'd better not be forgetting it: the missus took me in when I was sick, after my husband and young'uns had died. That sainted woman nursed me back to health when nobody else'd even come near me. I'd as lief kill you myself, right where you lay, afore I'll let you bring any more hurt to the missus.'

'I . . .'

'Boy, they tell me you're a man of your word. Can you swear to me that you ain't aiming to cause that poor soul any more pain?'

He wanted to swear, but if he broke the vow he made to his grandfather, was there any guarantee he would keep a new one? He hesitated only briefly before he said, 'No, Daisy, I can't.'

'Eat up, but consider yourself rightly warned. Something you said while you was raving keeps a-nagging at the back part of my mind. All that happened around here drove it deep, but I'll remember, and when I do . . . '

Hands clasped on top of her apron, she paused at the door to the other room and looked back over her shoulder at Rogue. 'Sooner or later, the memory will come back, and when it does . . . ' she let the words trail off before she walked out of the room, leaving Rogue with a new worry.

What had he said?

14

Daisy's angry warning and his own growing weariness had turned the food to sawdust, but Rogue made himself eat — even if the venison stew and sourdough bread seemed to stick in his throat. He had to regain his strength, but not knowing what he had said in his fevered dreaming was gnawing at him. Had he said who he was, what he intended for Odom? Had Faith heard? Or Deidre?

Not that it mattered now. Nothing had changed. The gang of outlaws, whoever they were, still waited somewhere in the rugged mountains, and they would close in for the kill. Dolph Odom was here. Rogue could still keep both promises, couldn't he?

No, nothing had changed, but for an instant he wished . . . Abruptly Rogue pushed that thought away. He walked alone, had no friends or family, and he had to keep it that way. His hands were stained with blood; he was Lejube Rogue, a demon who was empty of all caring. He wasn't fit to be a brother to those innocent kids. And he didn't want to, how could he even if . . .

He sighed, but it came out more like a moan.

'Are you hurting real bad, Mr. Rogue?' Faith asked, her young voice soft, filled with real concern.

Rogue jumped, almost dropping bowl, stew, and spoon as his muscles tensed, his free hand starting for the Colts. He stopped himself just in time, saved the venison, and stared at the girl standing at the foot of the bed. He didn't having an inkling how she got there. Had he been so lost in his misery that he hadn't even heard her come in? That scared him. She wasn't a danger, but when a man lives by his wits, he doesn't live long when he lets those wits go wandering.

It would have been easy to blame the

lapse on his weakness, but it wouldn't have been true. It was this family — the family he hadn't known of — that was getting to him, breaking down his defenses. If he didn't put a stop to it, they would destroy him — and they would never even know what they done.

The little girl stood there, a small figure in a starched calico dress, tugging at a neat plait of hair, looking at him with eyes full of caring. And Rogue knew she cared, and knew, too, that he had to put an end to it, had to turn her away — for her sake as well as his own. Glaring at her and hating himself for doing it, he snarled, 'What do you want?'

Her thin cheeks reddened under the freckles, but she didn't flinch or move away. 'I'm sorry,' she said. 'I know you must be hurting real bad, and it's all my fault. I really didn't mean to bother you, but . . . Your clothes were ruined. Daisy found some others in your pack and washed them and she . . . She's sort of grouchy, but . . . Do you need any more to eat or . . . '

'No.' He returned the bowl to the tray.

'I'm really sorry. I didn't want you to get shot,' she said as she placed his clothes on the foot of the bed and walked around to pick up the tray. 'I know you don't feel like it, but Mama wants to talk to you and . . . She's been sick for a long time and . . . '

'No, Faith, please. I can't . . . ' Rogue spoke with a growing urgency, but he was too late. Faith was already gone. Closing his eyes, telling himself he'd had worse trials before, Rogue waited and, almost against his will, his fingers came up to caress the medicine pouch that hung round his neck. Deidre's picture was there, still unchanged by the years, but Patrick Scanlon had changed. He had become a man of power's adopted son before the white priests had come for him, educated him in their schools. Somewhere beyond that time, he had become a killer, and now only Lejube Rogue remained of what had been.

Deidre wasn't long in coming. Slowly, tiredly, she walked into the gloomy, barely lit room. Her long plain dress was made of some soft, shimmery material, and it whispered gently as she came across the room and seated herself on the chair beside his bed.

For one terrible moment, Rogue wanted to put his head in her lap and weep away all his troubles. He wanted to be her little boy again with an intensity so great it carried pain — but it could never be. That little boy was gone, destroyed by the drunken old man this woman had given him to before she ran away with the man who had murdered her husband. Between them, Deidre and his grandfather had killed all innocence, all sweetness, and loosed a lonely demon to walk in that little boy's place. Now, when fate had brought them together, there was no way to bridge the years and the pain that set them apart. This woman was a stranger, a woman he would never know.

Mutely, her eyes searched his bruised face. She sat beside the bed for what seemed an eternity before tears welled up in her eyes and she asked, in a choked, barely audible voice, 'Who are you? For the love of a merciful and compassionate God, who are you?'

He wanted to say, 'Don't you know me, Mama? I'm Patrick Scanlon, your son,' but instead he said, 'They call me Rogue, ma'am, Lejube Rogue.'

She looked at him again, one hand reached out as if she intended to touch his face, trace the contours that were teasing at her memory, but she let it drop. 'In the Old Country, where my family came from, people with The Sight were honored, but 'tis not the same in this land. Here 'tis a curse. They think I'm mad, and perhaps I am, I dunna know.

'Sometimes The Sight comes upon me and I . . . but I would not have this seeing true. For a wee moment, you were my Patrick, my first-born, the lad I carried beneath my heart. But, I see you are not, could never be, my own sweet one. No, your face is of the hardness of marble. Your pale eyes are the icy-cold of death. Awww, sir, it hurts me, but you are an empty man, a man without peace or hope.

'I would ask your pardon for my words, but they are naught but true. I grieve for the life of sorrow that has made you thus, but I know you are never my son.'

She was still looking at him, and Rogue returned her stare. She had thrown him away long ago, and he owed her nothing, but something tugged at him — and that frightened him, made him want to ease her suffering, to forgive her everything, ask to be her son again. He couldn't. The time for that, if it ever had been, no longer existed.

'Oh, how silly I am,' she cried, sounding entirely different than she had just seconds before, 'and how thought-less. Faith told me not to come and visit you. She said you were feeling poorly, is that so, lad?'

'Just tired,' he said, wanting her gone before he betrayed himself.

'Faith takes too much upon her small shoulders, poor lass. She thinks highly of you, but she hasn't been herself since those men ... Perhaps 'tis only the nightmares that plague her, keep her from her sleep.

'Sir, it shouldn't have happened. She is still a child, a wee lass who should be playing with toys, not carrying the world. Children should only walk paths of safety and love. God gives us our precious wee ones to cherish and protect.'

Rogue agreed with what she was saying, but he couldn't say a word. She couldn't have thought her first-born was precious or needed love — she had given him to a man who knew only hate.

Deidre leaned close and spoke softly. 'My dear husband has said you must leave here as soon as you are able, but I will not let you go. I want you here. You aren't like the rest of them. You can kill them devils and not . . . Mr. Rogue, my children must be kept safe, and you can do it. I know I sound selfish and uncaring of your well-being, and perhaps I am. But what happens to you, or to me, doesn't really matter. We're evil, but my children are . . . Children shouldn't be punished for the sins of their parents.'

Bowing her head, she sat, looking down, twisting the material of her skirt between her thumb and forefinger. Finally, she spoke, her voice dull, lifeless, 'Those men will come back and when we can fight no more, they will kill . . . '

'No,' Rogue said grimly, 'they won't.'

She raised her head, looked beyond him, stared at something only she could see. 'The Sight has been passed down in my family for generations, and now it speaks . . . '

Rogue believed in power, knew in part what it could do, but he didn't want . . . 'No, ma'am,' he said softly, feeling some of his own power start to rise, 'they will never . . .'

'My husband doesn't . . . He will not . . . You must take my wee ones and slip away in the night, take them to the good father in Jacksonville. He will keep them safe.'

There was agony in her voice, in her eyes, but Rogue couldn't do what she asked. 'Faith and Robby will never be safe as long as one of those men are alive. I know what they planned to do to Faith, and no one sane would . . .'

As if she hadn't heard a single one of his words, Deidre interrupted with, 'Take them now! Tonight! You must! I see it! I see my son lying dead! I see it! Blood! Shooting! Killing! Blood! Blood everywhere!' Her voice rose higher and higher until she was almost screaming, keening an Irish lament for a loss that was yet to come.

Rogue touched her arm, and for a fleeting moment, he knew the full depths of her torture, saw the bloody horror of her vision, and wanted to embrace her. He wanted to hold her close, tell his mother she would never lose another son; instead, he shouted, 'Daisy! Daisy!' and patted his mother's clenched fists as he tried, ineffectively and with growing need, to soothe her. He shouted for Daisy again.

It wasn't Daisy who came in response to his frantic call; it was Dolph Odom. With Faith coming behind him, he ran into the room, went straight to his wife, lifted her up, held her close, and said, 'Don't, my dearest love, don't. Please, love, it's over. It was over long ago. You've cried enough.'

'My darling,' she whispered, 'I dinna mean to . . . 'Tis The Sight. It's come back to . . . My son will die, love, and I cannot . . . ' She sort of drooped against him, looked as if all her strength had drained away, leaving her nothing to sustain her but sorrow.

Odom lifted her, cradled her against his chest, and had eyes for no one else as he carried her out, whispering endearments, reassurances, and words of devotion. Faith watched them go before she came over to the bed, leaned against the back of the chair her mother had occupied, and asked, her voice holding more than a hint of a quaver, 'What happened to Mama?'

'I don't know,' Rogue answered. 'She was just fine and then . . . '

'I think it was what those men did to her graveyard that made her . . . She was sick like this before. And I just don't understand why she thinks God is punishing her for . . . She's so good, why would she think that she deserves to be punished by God or anybody else?'

'Because she . . . ' The truth was in Rogue's mouth, trying to rush out, but he stopped abruptly. What good could come of telling this child of her mother's acts, her desertion of her older son? He said instead, 'I know very little about women,' and it, too, was the truth.

'Did your mother . . . '

Again he resorted to a truth that was incomplete. 'My mother? I don't have a mother, Faith.'

'Is she . . . she dead?'

'Yes, as far as I'm concerned, I think she is.'

Faith's chin started to quiver, tears filled her eyes, and she whispered, 'I'm really sorry, Mr. Rogue.'

'Stop that,' he almost shouted. 'Don't you ever cry for me!' But even as he made the demand, somewhere deep within him, he wanted her, or someone, to care enough to cry for his hurts.

'I won't cry any more,' Faith said quietly, wiping away the telltale moisture with the back of her hand and trying to smile at him, and for that moment, she was more adult than he had ever been. She had a compassion and an understanding that would never be his.

'You rest,' she said, 'and I'll go help Daisy. Papa wants us to cook up a lot of food today so there won't be any fires burning if the outlaws come back after dark. And Mama won't be able to help now — she'll just sleep for a long time, and when she wakes up, she will just be Mama again. And, Mr. Rogue, please, don't feel bad about what happened — it wasn't your fault.'

She smiled at him, whirled around, and was almost to the inner door before she paused, looked back over her shoulder, and said, 'Don't worry about me. I won't cry any more. It doesn't really help much, does it?' She smiled again. It was a real smile, but it wasn't a child's smile.

The smile almost did him in. He, too, had been forced into adulthood before his time, and he knew the hurt. This child, his little sister, had to be protected from any more of that pain, even if he had to break the vow . . . No, this wasn't the time to think of that, of what it would do to Faith when he shot down her father, but he couldn't stop, couldn't do anything but lie there and watch her go.

'I've got to get out of here,' he

muttered. The words seemed to echo in the empty room, and he looked around a little too quickly. It hadn't taken much to spook him. Just a mother's cries of madness and a little girl's smile of love. That's all it took for a demon to know real fear.

Reaching down, he grabbed his gray wool pants from the stack of clothes and wiggled into them under the bed covers. He was panting and sweating by the time he had them up and buttoned, but now he could get up, walk around, and get some of his strength back without offending any of the females in the process.

His buckskin shirt was probably beyond repair, but there was a gray shirt in the pile, some new wool socks, but no moccasins. Rogue was pulling the shirt over his head when Dolph Odom came through the inner door and asked, 'You planning on going somewhere?'

Rogue had heard him coming, knew who it was before the big man had come into the room, but he saw no reason to answer. The shirt on, he swung his legs around, sat on the edge of the bed, and reached for the wool socks, all without saying a word.

'My wife isn't crazy, she has these spells and . . . Her family has always had some sort of . . . Well, maybe it's power or something, but it isn't there all the time, and . . . In time, when this is over, she will be as she was.'

Knowing he should say something, but not sure exactly what it should be, Rogue tugged on the thick socks and waited for Odom to say whatever it was he had come to say.

'Deidre wants you to stay. She begged me to ask, and I said I would.'

'Do you want me to stay?'

'No, I want you gone as soon as possible. I don't want a killer in my house.'

'Ah,' Rogue said softly, feeling his face take on the look folks had called wolfish, 'you're planning to go with me then?'

Odom bristled. 'What's that supposed to mean?'

'Just that you saying I can't stay in your house because I'm a killer makes for some mighty strange hearing, considering you killed my father. Am I sort of mixed up, or doesn't that make you a killer, too?.'

There was no fear in Odom's voice when he asked, 'One you've come to kill?'

Rogue stood up and looked at the man standing on the far side of the room, and his voice was equally calm and even when he asked, 'You know me then?'

15

The fire had died to ash and ember. The lamp guttered and smoked. Light stabbed through the shutters like swords of brightness in the gloom. But it wasn't dark, not really. Rogue had no trouble seeing Odom, seeing the guilt written plain in the other man's eyes, the guilt and something else — just what that something else was, Rogue couldn't know. He waited for the other man to answer the question, to acknowledge Rogue for who and what he was.

'Yes,' Odom said, 'I've known you since we found you half-dead in that rock pile, but, Rogue, I will never call you by that other name. My wife believes her son is dead and . . . do what you will, I'll not beg for mercy. Are you able to walk to the barn? We can do our fighting there, away from

Deidre's hearing. It's the sound of guns and the sight of blood that make her . . . '

'I'm not going to kill you now,' Rogue said, but he didn't add, 'And maybe I'm not going to kill you at all,' but the thought was there, creeping around inside his mind, tempting him down ways he couldn't walk.

'When?'

'I can't even think about it right now, Odom. With you or without you, I'm going to wipe out that gang from the canyon. I promised Faith that they would never touch her again. I intend to keep that promise before I worry about any others,' Rogue said slowly. He looked at Odom square, trying to read the expressions that were warring on the other man's face. Mostly, he guessed, it was growing fear and some kind of horror.

'That gang? It's not yours? One you brought with you to finish what was . . . '

'Whatever was in the past, I am truly

Lejube Rogue now, and I ride alone.'

'But Ben said ... I thought you ... Dear God, what have I done? Who are they then? What do they want from me?'

Rogue shrugged. 'I don't know.'

Taking several steps in Rogue's direction, Odom said, his voice hoarse, 'I don't either. My family ... Rogue, my guilt made me blind and ... I have put them in terrible danger. You owe me nothing, but I ask because you are her son, will you stay and help me protect your mother?'

'I reckon she gave up that claim a long time ago, and she's nothing to me now. Your wife is just a poor, sad woman, but Faith is something else. I'll stay for her, and for Robby.'

Odom nodded. 'And what's between us will wait until this other is over?'

'As far as I'm concerned. Is that straight with you?'

The older man nodded. Pain giving him a few reminders that he had been shot, Rogue limped to where Odom stood and held out his hand to seal the bargain.

'And it's just between us. No one else needs to know?'

Rogue answered, 'Between us.'

Their hands met, the pact was sealed, but they both knew that if they managed to defeat the outlaws, then their own meeting was inevitable. They would meet, guns would blaze, and only one of them would walk away.

There seemed to be nothing more to say, but Odom asked, 'What's Ben got against you? Have you had trouble with him somewhere else?'

'No. As far as I know, I've never laid eyes on him before coming here.'

The rancher looked troubled. He started to say something more, but the door to the outside opened, sending in a fan of light, followed by Shorty and Haskins, each carrying bedrolls and a few other things. The door was still closing behind them when Shorty asked, 'Where are you aiming on us a-bunking, Boss?'

'In here, with Rogue. When you get time, bring his moccasins and his carbine. If those men come again tonight, he'll need them.'

'He's staying?'

'Yes. Where's Robby? And Ben?'

Dropping his bedroll onto the floor, Shorty answered, 'Robby's a-watching for them dog-killers just like you told him. Ben's still out in the bunkhouse, getting his gear ready to ride out. He ain't a-saying much to the likes of us, but I reckon he'll be coming in right shortly.'

'I'll go find him,' Odom said, giving Rogue a quick look before he stepped around his hired hands and jerked open the door.

Rogue didn't watch him go. Pain was shooting up his leg, making him sway where he stood, but he had to limber it up, get some strength back into it. Steeling himself, he walked to the fireplace, across to the water bucket, and back to the bed. He was moving slow by the time he got there and welcomed the comfort of the caned-bottom chair when he eased himself down. He was light-headed and pain was burning hot in his chest, but he had done better than he would have thought possible — almost he wondered if the dreams of Eagle Flying had had something to do with his rapid healing.

But he didn't dwell on the subject. Instead he asked, partly out of curiosity and partly because the power was still within him and its ways weren't easily understood, 'Shorty, have you known Odom very long?'

'Long enough, I reckon. His pa, the rich Mr. James Buskirk Odom, took me away from my ma when I wasn't more'n a tadpole. I slept on a pallet in front of Mr. Dolph's floor 'til we was both too old for it to be . . . That's where I got my name, from his pa,' Shorty said, and the bitterness in his voice was almost thick enough to cut with a knife. 'Boy, I don't know why you're a-asking, but, yeah, I knowed him man and boy.'

234

'I didn't mean to pry, but I have to know something, and you're the only one I know to ask,' Rogue said, giving the man the apology he thought he owed him.

'I know that, son, so just do your asking. James Buskirk Odom is long dead anyways, and hating don't do much to change what was.'

'Shorty, who has it in for Odom? I mean who hates him enough to sic that pack of outlaws on him?'

'I dunno nothing about 'um, Rogue. Odom's a hard man, but he's fair. Maybe them owlhoots are just crazy.'

'Maybe so,' Rogue answered, but he doubted it. There had to be a reason. Finding it was the problem. That, and getting his strength back. He stood up again, made a slow circuit of the room, and stopped at the water bucket long enough to drink a dipper of water. He made it back to the chair in time to watch Shorty poke up the fire and add wood. The flames leapt high, adding new brightness to the room.

He didn't ask what they were doing. Rogue just watched when Shorty and Haskins, talking too quiet for him to hear, took out their knives, whetted them to sharp edge, and began whittling long curls from the boards they had evidently brought in with their bedding.

They were quiet, intent on what they were doing, and Rogue was equally intent on his own affairs. The thing with Odom had been settled for awhile, so he didn't need to worry it any more. But the other problem was still deadly, and he couldn't do much about it until he was strong enough to go snake hunting. That came first.

Standing up, he took another walk, making it around the room twice before weakness sent sweat popping out on his forehead and him back to the chair. He was just getting his breathing under control when Odom came in, trailed by Ben.

Odom started talking before he was well into the room. 'Rogue,' he said,

'Ben needs a little more information before he goes down to Eagle Point to hire some guns. Do you feel up to answering a few questions?'

Rogue nodded.

'Faith insists that there were thirty or forty men in the canyon, is that about right?'

Before Rogue could answer, Ben broke in with, 'Boss, I ain't a-calling Faith no kind of liar, but she sure does like to build things up in that little head of hers. She's just a kid, and I figger she was scared some, and . . . '

Without a single glance in Ben's direction, Rogue said, 'Faith did a real good job of counting. There's probably thirty-five or so of them now. We killed some, and they were having a few problems when we left.'

Only then did he turn to Ben. He said, letting every bit of the coldness he felt creep into his voice and turn it to black, unyielding ice, 'Ben, I don't know what your stake is in this game, but I'm warning you now, don't ever

237

call Faith names. I don't like it.'

His eyes narrowing to slits, Ben's right hand began to inch toward the shiny gun belted to his hip.

Knowing it was what folks called his demon smile, Rogue let his face grow hard, his lips move in a narrow imitation of a smile. 'Ben,' he said, 'I would take great pleasure in killing you, if that's what you're asking for. If Mr. Odom will oblige me by reaching over on the bed and handing me my Colts, I'll be real happy to fulfill . . . '

Odom turned on Ben. 'What in the hell do you think you're doing?' he asked, his voice sounding mean.

Ben wilted. 'Boss,' he whined, 'I didn't aim to shoot. The skunk is just trying to push me into a gunfight. He's in with those outlaws, and he damned sure doesn't want me going down to the valley and hiring any help. And, Boss, I reckon you think that, too.'

'You're wrong there,' Odom answered. 'I know Rogue, and he isn't with anyone. He came here on his own business, and he's staying because I asked him. Remember that.'

''Pears to me you changed your tune a mite. What's he been telling you? He's a damned liar if he said anything about me, and I'll . . . ' He balled his fists and took a single step toward Odom. Rogue could almost smell his fear — but he didn't know the cause of it. That worried him.

Odom returned his foreman's stare and said, 'Go out to the corral and drop a loop on that big roan. Work the kinks out of him. By the time you're finished, both of you should be feeling real peaceful.'

'But . . . '

'You heard me. Go.'

'Yeah, Odom, I heard you. And I reckon you're gonna be mighty sorry for this,' Ben said, and to Rogue's ears it sounded an awful lot like a threat.

It must have sounded the same to Odom. He faced Ben, asked, 'Just what do you mean by that, Ben?'

'Nothing, Boss. I reckon I just meant

skunks should be shot where you find 'um, but he's your skunk, ain't he?' Ben smiled and swaggered out, leaving only silence behind him.

Rogue pushed himself up, tried to stand, but sitting had caused his leg to stiffen. It gave beneath his weight; he almost fell. Moving quickly for a big man, Odom grabbed his arm and held him up. 'Don't be a fool, Rogue. Go back to bed and let yourself heal up some before you bite off more than you can chew,' he said, his voice a little gruff.

'I can't wait. Those killers will likely be back tonight, and I have to be able to move around when they come.' He pulled away from Odom's grip and began another slow, limping walk around the room. Odom didn't say anything more, but he walked beside Rogue ready to give help if it was needed.

Carrying a pine board that had been carved, Shorty met them in the center of the floor. He gave Rogue a quick, almost furtive look before he gave his full attention to Dolph Odom. 'Boss,' he said, 'it ain't much, but me and Haskins figgered the missus might feel some better if she knew we was a-gonna do something about her little graveyard. We thought we'd just get a head start and have these markers done when . . . you think these dates are right?'

He held out the marker. It read:

R.I.P.

Patrick Scanlon

b. July 1, 1850

d. May 10, 1855

He had heard them talking about the graveyard, remembered Faith talking about her brother and the babies who were buried there, but the truth of it hadn't touched him until that very moment. Staring at the rough marker, he swayed, reached out blindly.

'Grab him, Boss, he's a-falling,' Shorty yelled. A strong arm went around Rogue, held him upright. He could feel hands gripping him, hear voices speaking, but he didn't know for sure what was being said. Lejube Rogue, the white Indian, felt like a mule had kicked him in the head, and it wasn't just his weakness that had brought him down.

His thoughts were muddled. The grave marker had been for Patrick Scanlon's grave, but if Patrick Scanlon, Deidre's first-born son was buried in that lonely little cemetery, then who was Rogue? Who had the old man raised as his grandson?

16

Shock, weakness, or maybe the power held him in its thrall, refused him speech and motion. Helpless for the moment, Rogue let the men drag him over to the bed, and he obeyed when they told him to lie down.

'Rest,' Shorty said, and Rogue could see his worried face peering down at him. It wavered hazily, but his seeing was no more muddled and mixed-up than his thinking — and one thing was growing clearer by the second: *Shorty had shown him that grave marker on purpose, but why?*

Shorty lifted him up, held the water dipper to his lips, and said, 'Drink. It's good for what ails you.' Rogue swallowed, but when the rim of the dipper left his lips, he looked at the puncher and asked, 'Why? Why did you . . . '

Leaning close, pretending to be

straightening Rogue's pillows, Shorty whispered, 'The grave's empty, boy.' He stepped back and said, 'I reckon he just over did a mite, so he's a-gonna take a little rest now, and we can do all the jawing that needs doing when he wakes up. Right, boy?'

Knowing Shorty intended to tell him something but was going to do it in his own way and in his own time, Rogue nodded and closed his eyes. He did sleep, but not well. His troubled thoughts took on new guises and followed him into a fitful, dream-plagued doze. He dreamed of Enos Scanlon, his grandfather, and dreamed once again of Eagle Flying.

The last dream seemed a true one. Eagle Flying, his face wrinkled, his eyes blind, seemed to be looking for Rogue, or maybe just needing to tell him something. He asked, 'Little brother, you have the power, why don't . . . '

'Help me, I don't understand.'

'Where are . . . '

'I need you, Eagle Flying.'

'Little brother, I can't . . . You must not fight . . . Yes, now I see. I will come.' The old shaman was gone, and Rogue was in a stifling hot room in the Cascade Mountains. He was awake, he was soaking wet with sweat, and he was still bemused, on the far edge of understanding what was happening to him.

Feeling the presence of someone else, but not a single forewarning of danger, Rogue opened his eyes.

Holding a wet cloth in her hand, Faith stood beside the bed looking down at him. She asked, 'You were talking again — was Eagle Flying good to Patrick?'

It caught him unaware, and he answered before he had time to think. 'Yes. Very good.'

She smiled at Rogue, smiled at her brother. 'I'm glad someone was. That awful old man hurt you enough.'

'You know?' The question was uttered half in hope, half in fear, and he wasn't sure which was the more important.

Her answer wasn't direct, but it held

something that added to his fear, and Rogue wasn't sure if his fear was for himself or for this little girl who had found her way into his heart.

'You saved my life, and I made them let me sit with you while you were sick. Daisy did some at night, but I did most. You talked a lot and . . . I hear lots of things. I heard you and Papa and . . . ' With nothing but trust in her eyes, Faith smiled at him. 'You're not really going to kill him, are you?' It wasn't really a question.

Rogue stared at her. 'Please, Faith, don't . . . I'm not what you think. I've done terrible . . . '

'Does that make any difference in who you are?' she asked, and before he could answer, she said, 'Daisy said to wash your hands and face. Supper's ready.'

'Faith, please, don't . . . '

She refused to listen. 'Daisy said that if you wouldn't wash, she'd come and do it for you. You'd better mind her, Rogue, she's really mean.'

Knowing he was beaten, Rogue held out his hand. Faith dropped the wet cloth in it. 'I'll go get the tray,' she said, grinning at him, 'and you'd better eat a lot, or she's likely to come and feed you, too.'

'Oh, I will,' Rogue said gruffly, but he could feel the beginnings of a smile tugging at his own lips.

Daisy brought the tray, left without saying a word, and Rogue sat up and ate with a growing hunger. By the time he had finished the venison steak, biscuits, gravy, and dried apple pie, the other men were back. Robby was with his father and the two punchers, but Ben wasn't.

Shorty and Haskins walked over to inspect Rogue. 'Well, son, you look a heap and a whole lot better,' Shorty said. Haskins, picking his teeth with a splinter of wood, nodded in agreement.

Something about Ben's absence nagged at him. From the looks of the light filtering in through the shutters, it wasn't full dark yet but was getting close. Ben was supposed to ride out after dark and . . . 'Has Ben left?' Rogue asked.

'Nope, he's a-taking a nap. There's a big storm building and . . . ' Shorty answered as he walked over to the outer door and pulled it open. 'Boss,' he said, 'maybe we'd better go get Ben now. He's gonna be in for it. Them thunderheads are pert near on us, and they're blacker than the inside of a black cat. It's gonna be a dandy.'

As if to verify his words, thunder growled — not too close, but close enough to tell them it was coming, and coming real soon.

Rogue turned to watch as Odom joined Shorty at the door. Both men stepped out, leaving the door open, giving Rogue his first glimpse of the broad porch that fronted the log house. Still talking about Ben, the two men walked across the rough boards and moved out of Rogue's sight.

Robby asked, 'Mr. Rogue, what do you think of Ben?'

The prickles started and ranged up Rogue's back and neck, and the feeling of danger was so strong it felt as if his hair was standing on end. 'I don't know what to think,' he said slowly, and that much was true.

'He hates Faith,' Robby said, coming closer, speaking softer. 'He's been saying some awfully rough things about her and to her. I talked to Papa and . . . They had some words this afternoon out in the barn, so I don't know if Ben's going to go down to the valley or not.'

'Rogue, boy, I'm a-thinking you'd better be getting yourself well in a hell of . . . ' A loud clap of thunder killed whatever else Haskins was going to say. Lightning flashed, lit the room; thunder crashed before it faded.

Violent, deadly, the storm hit. The house shook. Lightning flashed again and again. The heavy bellow of thunder was constant, deafening. Speech was impossible.

It seemed an eternity before Odom

and Shorty ran in through the open door. Odom shouted, 'Is Ben in here?'

His question was barely audible over the storm. Rogue shook his head.

'Did you hear a shot?'

Again Rogue shook his head.

'He's gone,' Odom said, and his words, too loud, came stark and clear in a sudden lull in the storm.

Thunder crashed again. Wind surged, howled.

Shutters banged. Something heavy fell. Hail bigger than grapes slashed down. Wind grabbed the icy pellets, slammed them across the porch.

It grew darker and the sky turned to yellow-green murk. Lightning sizzled. Thunder clapped before the blue-white flash was gone. Hail pelted and bounced, piled in wind-driven drifts.

'Boss, it hit something out back,' Haskins yelled.

'Damnation!' Odom sprinted for the inner door and through it. Shorty and Haskins weren't more than a step behind.

Lightning flashed again, farther away. The hail turned to rain. A spatter at first, then a deafening roar. The wind shifted, rushed through the open door, and scoured the stuffy heat from the room. It brought the rich sweet smell of wet earth and a coolness that came close to being a chill — or maybe it was just the icy warning on the back of Rogue's neck that made him shiver.

Listening intently, almost holding his breath, Rogue tried to turn a mewling sound into something recognizable, something that didn't scream of danger. Pulling one of the loaded Colts from its holster, Rogue stood up. His leg gave a sharp twinge, but he had no time for weakness. He eased past the bed and, six-gun ready, he moved to the open door, peeked around the edge, looked out into the raging storm.

A man was crawling across the rough-sawn boards of the porch floor, leaving a trail of red in the slushy drifts of melting hail.

'Robby, get your father. Quick!'

Rogue shouted. He scanned the yard, examined everything that might conceal even a hint of trouble. The storm clouds were tree-top low and blue-black with wetness. The curtain of pounding rain hid everything more than thirty feet from the door. He couldn't see a single living thing, except the wounded man — a man who definitely was not Ben.

Odom came up behind him, touched his shoulder, hissed, 'What's the matter?'

Rogue pointed with the gun barrel.

Odom didn't waste time asking questions. 'Cover me,' he said. Crouching, he ran out on the porch, grabbed the stranger by the shoulders, and dragged him into the room.

Thunder rumbled and echoed. Lightning flashed close.

Thunder crashed. Odom shouted, 'Bar the door, Robby.'

The boy ran to obey while Odom turned the crawling man face-up on the puncheon floor. Rogue winced when he saw the wound. The man's hands came up and clutched his belly, and he moaned. Blood seeped redly from between his spread fingers.

'Who is he? One of the outlaws?' Robby asked.

'I don't know, but he's hurt bad. Get Daisy. Shorty is checking the summer kitchen for fire. Call him. Bring some clean rags and some warm water,' Odom ordered, scarcely looking up from the man on the floor.

The room was filled with gloom, was dusky dark, but Rogue had no trouble recognizing the man. He knew that face. It was Kale, the man from the canyon, the man who had taken his gold and ran. But why had he come back?

Kale mumbled. 'Big man? Little girl? Hafta find. Hafta find. Danger. Hafta find.'

'You're all right now,' Odom said. 'Don't try to talk, there'll be plenty of time for that when we get you patched up.

It wasn't true. From the looks of his wound, Kale would be lucky if he lived through the night. And, from the sound of things, Rogue owed him for something — just what that was, he wasn't sure, but it was pretty obvious that Rogue and Faith were who he was looking for.

Before he could say anything, Shorty and Haskins came in, Shorty carrying another lamp, one with a clean, unsmoked chimney. Haskins took one look at the man on the floor and said, 'My God, he's been gut-shot. Who did it?'

Eyes glazed with pain, Kale looked up, stared blankly, and finally said, 'Ben. Ben Butler shot me. Took my horse. Shot me.'

Muttering as darkly as the storm, Daisy came stomping in, elbowed Haskins out of the way, dropped the rags she was carrying, and groaned as she tried to get down on her knees beside the man.

The power rose high and made

Rogue step forward. It made him say as gently as possible, 'Let me,' and it made him kneel at Kale's side.

'You're going to heal him, aren't you? Like you did me?' Robby asked as he sat a basin of water on the floor in front of Rogue. 'Do you need that bag of yours? The beaded one?'

At Rogue's nod, Robby said, 'Now you'll see I wasn't lying,' and ran to do Rogue's bidding.

Daisy snorted. 'Damn fool, just like all men. He ain't got a Chinaman's chance. Leave 'um be.'

'Can you really do something?' Odom asked. 'I don't know who he is or why he's here. But even if he's one of the outlaws, he doesn't deserve to die like that.'

'I can ease him, take away some of the pain, but in the end he will . . . '

Nodding to show he understood what Rogue was telling him, Odom turned away and walked over to the shuttered window. He stood there for a moment before he asked, 'He was looking for you, you and Faith, wasn't he? To warn you about something?'

'That's what it sounds like, but . . . '

'Ben,' Odom said slowly. 'Ben Butler? He has to be related to the rustlers we hung, but . . . '

Remembering something he had heard in the canyon, Rogue said, 'I think he's the nephew the outlaws were talking about. The old man's nephew. Faith said the old man looked like a spider, all bent and . . . '

Odom nodded, but before any more could be said, Robby returned, handed Rogue his bag, and said, 'If you need anything else, I'll . . . '

'Thanks,' Rogue said. Then, ignoring everything and everyone except the task at hand, he cleaned the wound and took a handful of the pungent mixture from the bag. The chant for healing spilled from his mouth, and he didn't know that he chanted aloud.

He ground the leaves and herbs between his two hands and sprinkled the resultant powder into the gaping wound. He took another large handful, ground it, mixed it with water, and spread a thick layer of the brown paste on a clean white cloth. The bleeding had stopped when Rogue spread the poultice over the bullet-torn flesh. He knew the medicine would ease the pain, but he couldn't lift the man and bind the wound alone. The chant died away. He looked up, said, 'I need some help now.'

Robby nodded, but Haskins, Shorty, and Daisy stood stiff, staring, some emotion strong in their eyes. 'You damned heathen, you'll get no help from me,' Daisy snarled, her voice thick with loathing, heavily laced with raw fear.

'Tell me what to do, I'll do it if I can,' Faith said softly. Rogue hadn't heard her come in, but when he looked at her, he saw nothing of fear, nothing of hate. Her expression was the same as her brother's: trusting, and a little proud.

'No, you won't.' Daisy grabbed the

child's thin arm, jerked her away from Rogue. 'You little fool, ain't you got no sense at all? You ain't got no business in here with this . . . this Injun. Get out and stay out!' The woman jerked Faith again, more roughly. Faith stumbled, almost fell. Daisy pulled her up, off her feet, and left her dangling from one arm. The little girl's face went white, twisted with pain, but she didn't make a sound.

Rogue did. He looked at the plump woman, knew there was nothing but ice in his eyes, in his voice when he said, 'Turn her loose. Do it now, and don't ever put your hands on her again.'

If Faith's arm had been a rattlesnake, Daisy couldn't have released it any quicker. 'Filthy breed,' she said, spitting out the words, 'Don't you dare talk to a decent, God-fearing woman like that! You mess with me, boy, and I'll shoot a hole through your stinking gut and . . .'

'Go back to the kitchen, Daisy,' Odom said quietly. 'I don't believe we 'need you any longer.'

'Men! Even you. Treat the missus like . . . '

'Go now before you say something you'll regret.'

'Men! Devils, every damned one of you!' she retorted, glaring at Odom before she turned and waddled out of the room.

17

No one watched Daisy go. Robby said, 'I'll help,' but Shorty stopped him, coming forward to kneel beside Kale as he said, 'No, you ain't strong enough. Haskins, you come over here and get on the other side of this here fella. We've got to lift him some so's Rogue can bind him real tight.'

Haskins hesitated, took a step back, away from Rogue. Odom made some sort of sound — it could have been a sigh — and walked over, knelt, slid one hand under Kale's shoulder, the other under his hip. Shorty did the same. They lifted the man. Rogue wound long strips of cloth around the middle of the limp body. When he had finished, the other two eased Kale back down onto the floor.

After a moment, the outlaw tensed, moaned softly, and opened his eyes, looked straight up at Rogue, and did a little sighing of his own. 'Thank God, it's you. I've been a-looking. Wanted to tell. Didn't run out on our deal. They caught me before I could . . . I didn't tell 'um about you and the little girl. They was real jumpy and brought me down to the other camp. It's about a mile from here.'

He closed his eyes, sort of shuddered, and said faintly, 'Big fight today. They killed Slim. More, too. Ben Butler shot me. Works here. Careful. They . . . dynamite. Gonna blow up . . . Gold in the canyon. Lots of . . . Save the little girl. She . . . ' He went limp, lay still, breathing heavy and starting to shake.

Getting to his feet with a slowness that came as a surprise, Rogue felt all used up, empty, but it was a good sort of empty — one he hadn't felt in a long time. Pain burned through the full length of his leg, but he could bear it. He walked around the room, his limp barely hampering him, trying to loosen the stiff muscle. Shorty and Odom just watched, but Haskins backed away when Rogue came close, fear twisting his face into a grimace.

It wasn't the first time it had happened, but for some reason Rogue noticed it more. Faith came to walk at his side; after a few steps she reached out, took his hand and asked, 'You helped Kale's pain go away. Does it matter what people like Haskins and Daisy think about you? Does it make any difference?'

Rogue had to smile. 'No, it doesn't, not a bit.'

She gave his hand a quick squeeze before she released it, ran to her father, and said, 'I'll go take care of Mama, but you'd better wrap Kale up. He's shivering.'

'Kale? Faith, do you know . . . '

'He was with the outlaws, but he came here to help us. Isn't that enough?'

'More than enough.' Odom smiled down at her, touched the top of her head with his forefinger, and said, 'Run along, honey, but stay away from Daisy for a little while. She was afraid, she didn't really mean what she said about . . .'

'She meant it, Papa, but don't worry, it's all right.'

She was gone almost before she finished the sentence.

Shorty talked Haskins and Robby into helping him lift Kale onto Rogue's bed. Odom waited until Rogue came near and said, 'I have to talk to you about that man, what you did.'

'Why?' Rogue started to move on.

'I told you, Papa,' Robby put in, 'but you wouldn't listen to me. I told you Rogue was a healer, but you . . .'

'Robby, I don't want to hear any more about this. Take a slicker and go up to the watch tower. And make damned sure you keep that rifle dry.'

'Yes, sir,' the boy said, giving Rogue a single despairing look before he did as he was told.

Odom didn't even watch him leave.

He asked, 'That man you saved, he was from the canyon, wasn't he?'

'Yes.'

'He said, 'Ben Butler. The old man's nephew.' We hung two of the Butler brothers, so that must mean Nash Butler didn't die. He's still alive and . . .'

'That sounds about right.'

'Ben was here, spying on us the whole time, and like a fool, I made him foreman and . . . ' Odom shook his head.

Shorty came over to where they stood. 'Looks like we're in for some big trouble, Boss, iffen what that fella said about Ben be true.'

'I've treated the whole situation too lightly. I thought someone else was . . . I thought it was meant just to frighten me and . . . We'll just have to fort up here and . . . '

The rain lessened, became a murmur. The storm sounded like it was moving off to the south. Thunder grumbled in the distance. Odom didn't seem to notice. He walked away from Rogue and Shorty, went to the fireplace, leaned his elbows on the mantle, hid his face in his hands, and stood with his back to the room.

Haskins moved around, cleaning up some of the mess that Rogue's doctoring had left, but Shorty stayed where he was, looking at Odom, and after a moment, he said, 'He's a-making plans, I reckon. But, he's a right proud man, Rogue. It hurts him some to know he made a mistake, one that might get us all killed.'

'Don't worry about it on my account, Shorty,' Rogue said and started to walk on. Shorty put a hand on his arm, stopped him, leaned close, and said, talking real quiet, 'I know who you are, son, and what you've come to do. I just want to tell you that Dolph Odom is a proud man and a hard one, but I reckon I think more a-him than I do of any other soul who walks the face of the earth. I'm telling you straight out, I don't want nothing to happen to him.'

'But it will,' Rogue said quietly. 'When this is over, then I will do what I have to do. Odom knows it, and so do I.'

'And you'll be a-making a big mistake. Odom's done a heap of things wrong, but he didn't kill your pa.'

'Lies won't save him.'

The black wrangler glanced toward his boss, looked back at Rogue. 'I ain't lying, son. I was there when it happened. I cain't talk now. I dunno, maybe I never can. I need to do a heap a-thinking on it and . . . '

A shot sounded.

Robby's shout came at the same time. 'They're coming!'

Lead thunked into the log walls. Men shouted. Cursed. Laughed, wildly, drunkenly. More weapons fired. More lead slammed into the building.

It seemed to happen all at once, so quickly that Rogue didn't have time to think about what Shorty had said. There was only time to rush to the bed, pick up his gunbelts, and buckle them around his hips. That done, he drew the Colts, spun the cylinders, and checked the loads.

'Odom,' he said, 'I hope you've got a lot of ammunition. It looks like it's going to be a very long night.'

Haskins looked at Rogue's six-shooters and asked, a quaver making his voice high, 'What're you aiming to do?'

'Shoot back.'

'But, we ain't a-been fighting with 'um. They just shoot some and leave. Likely, we ain't got no call to . . . '

Rogue ignored him, went to the window, and peeked through the wooden shutter. The glass pane beyond the heavy wood reflected the yellow glow of the lamps, allowing not a glimpse of anything else.

'Douse the lights,' he ordered. Someone obeyed. Rogue rammed the gun barrel through the gun loop and into the window glass. It shattered, fell with a noisy tinkling. I'm not sure I believe this — they've been under attack for several days, and the glass hasn't been shot out?

Haskins said, 'Why'd you hafta do that? We packed that glass all the way from Jacksonville. The missus is a-gonna be right mad, and I don't blame her.'

'Haskins, shut your fool mouth and go out to the kitchen,' Odom said shortly. 'Make sure those shutters are barred. Shoot at anything that tries to get in. Shorty, you stay here with Rogue and do what you have to do. I'm going up to the tower. I'll send Robby down here where it's a little safer.'

Nodding, Rogue waited until his eyes had adjusted to the heavy gloom outside the cabin. Horsemen loomed large in the dark, galloping back and forth, shooting and yelling. He aimed at a rider, led him a little, and fired. The man screamed and fell. Rogue fired again. This man didn't scream: he was dead before he hit the soggy ground.

Shorty's handgun blasted. Rogue didn't see anyone fall.

The Colt in Rogue's hand bucked. Another outlaw tumbled from his horse. He crawled away. A dark trail marked his passage.

Shorty fired again. A thin, bearded man rode on with more than half of his face gone. Then he fell, jerked once, and was still.

As Rogue watched, the mounted men drew back out of pistol range. Still yelling curses, they pulled their rifles from their saddle scabbards and renewed shooting, firing volley after deadly volley at the house.

Lead splatted against a shutter, ripped through, and showered the room with splinters of wood.

Glass crashed in another window.

A slug hit the stones of the fireplace, ricocheted, dug a long gash in the opposite wall.

'They're getting a mite cantankerous, ain't they?' Shorty called, hunkering down under his window, using the thick logs of the wall for a shield.

Moving carefully, Robby crouched

down, came to Rogue, and handed him a rifle. 'Use this. It shoots a little to the left and about two inches high at a hundred yards.'

His Colts reholstered, Rogue nodded his thanks, took the weapon from the boy, and took aim. Centering the bead in the iron sight, he found a target and squeezed the trigger. Another outlaw spilled his blood on the earth.

He looked for another invader — there were none. The gang of attackers had backed off, were hidden in a stand of trees, almost as if they were hiding from something more than just Rogue's shooting.

Before Rogue had more than a second or two to wonder about the oddity of their actions, sound roared, thundered, and blasted through the night. The sky turned red, blood red, fire red.

'My God, what was that?' Shorty gasped.

Neither Rogue nor Robby had an answer.

Fire fell from the sky. Sizzled. Fought with the mist of falling rain.

Fiery brands and heavier debris thunked and clattered on the roof. Fell in the yard. Smoldered. Smoked.

The sky grew orange-red, brighter.

'It's hell-fire!' Daisy screamed, her voice coming from somewhere beyond the inner door. 'Hell-fire. Raining down. We're all gonna die! God is a-punishing us for taking in that filthy heathen. That demon straight out of Hell. Kill him!'

'Hush,' Haskins said, his voice not much quieter and just as scared. 'Do you want him to hear you?'

'You yella skunk, God will damn you for this!' the woman shrieked before she started moaning and sobbing and praying, all at the top of her voice, drowning out Haskins as he tried to calm her.

It was always the same. Rogue was tempted to sigh, but he smiled thinly and asked, 'Where's the barn?'

Robby answered, 'Out in back.

271

About where the fire is, I think. What did they do?'

'Dynamite,' Kale said, his voice weak, but holding no trace of pain. 'Blew it up. Tomorrow. Gonna blow up the house. Lots of dynamite down . . . ' His words slurred, faded into silence.

'Odom!' a man shouted from somewhere outside. 'Odom!' he shouted again, and then he laughed, a high-pitched whinnying giggle that sent shivers down Rogue's spine.

'Come out and look at your pretty barn, Odom. Listen to your horses. They like my fire. They're still in there, a-screaming for more.'

'That bastard! That crazy bastard,' Shorty almost sobbed.

In the quiet that followed, they listened hard, but all they could hear was fire noise, Daisy crying, and the man's insane laughter.

'Odom,' the unseen man called, 'your family is gonna go next. We're gonna burn 'um, so's you can hear 'um a-screaming when the fire eats 'um.' He laughed again.

Going in turn to each of the room's four windows, Rogue searched for even the slightest glimpse of the man. He was nowhere in sight. 'Where's he hiding, Shorty?'

'I dunno for sure. Sounds like . . . maybe those oaks in the back.'

'Can Haskins see him?'

'I reckon — iffen he's a-looking.'

Frustrated, angry that Faith was having to live through what was happening, Rogue allowed some of his anger to show. 'Why doesn't Haskins shoot?'

'Don't be hard on him, son. He's a cow puncher, and he ain't real used to killing. I reckon he's scared plumb out of his boots. Poor devil ain't no kind of hand with a gun, and . . . You want I should ease in there and see if I can get off a shot?'

'No, not . . . Where's Odom?'

'Up in the tower. We built it a while back when there was talk of . . . '

'Can he see . . .'

'I reckon he can. The tower's on top of the house, and it's open all the way 'round, but them trees and the summer kitchen hides a bit.'

'Papa's a careful shot,' Robby said. 'He'll wait until he's pretty sure of . . .'

A rifle cracked.

The man laughed, higher and wilder. 'You missed, Odom, but you won't miss your family burning.' Again he laughed. The rest of the gang laughed, too, as they shouted curses and threats. And once again their rifles came into the action, pumping lead into the thick logs of the house walls.

Bullets thudded or whined away. Men screamed with laughter, screamed warnings of impending doom.

'We'll be back!'

'You wait right here.'

'Fire!'

Their laughter was loud, drifting back after them as they rode off into the night.

'Are they all crazy?' Robby asked,

274

fear heavy in his voice.

'Drunk,' Kale said. 'Whiskey and gold. What the old man gives 'um. They killed Slim. Blood everywhere. Was going to kill me.'

The glow from the still burning barn filtered into the room, made moving around a lot less troublesome. After a final look out the window, Rogue went to the bed, sat down beside the wounded man. 'Kale,' he asked, 'is there anything more I can do for you?'

'No, I don't reckon so,' Kale answered, and then he asked, his voice real quiet, 'I'm a-cashing in my chips, ain't I?'

Rogue couldn't lie. 'Yes,' he said, knowing mere words could do nothing to soften the blow. 'I did what I could, but . . . Easing your pain was all . . . I'm truly sorry.'

18

Kale looked at Rogue and gave him a small smile. 'Ain't no need for sorrowing, mister. You treated me right good, and I ain't hurting none. Just kinda weak and fadey-like. Anyways, I reckon I wouldn't be a-wanting to ride out without old Slim there a-taking care of me.'

'Is there anyone you want told?'

The dying outlaw mumbled something and then said, 'Naw, there ain't nobody left that gives a damn. But that Ben Butler is a mean son and . . . Well, I'd take it real kindly if you'd shoot him a-fore he does any more harm.'

Rogue didn't hesitate. 'I'll do that if I can.'

Kale's voice was noticeably weaker when he asked, 'And you'll take care of that lil' girl?'

'I can promise you that.'

'Mister, you was good to me. Ain't many men I can say that about. I'd die real peaceful if you'd give me your name. I got me a notion who you are, but . . . '

Rogue shifted on the edge of the bed and cleared his throat. 'You guessed right, back on the canyon rim,' he said. 'I'm Rogue. Lejube Rogue.'

'I'm right honored to know you, sir,' Kale said, his voice not much more than a hoarse whisper. 'I heard a right smart about you, but . . . '

Shorty came to the bed. 'He's using too much of his strength, Rogue. He needs to be resting and . . . '

Rogue shook his head. 'No, he needs to say whatever needs saying while he still has time to do it.'

'But, I thought you . . . Robby said you were going to heal him and . . . '

'I would have, if it had been possible, but I could do nothing but give him some ease,' Rogue answered, not even trying to hide the regret in his voice.

'Well, I reckon he's going easy, and

277

that's something.'

'Iffen you was in my place, you'd think it was a whole hell of lot,' Kale whispered.

'Sorry,' Shorty said, his voice not much louder than the dying man's. 'I didn't mean to . . . '

Ignoring the puncher's stuttering attempt at an apology, Rogue asked, 'Kale, you said something about gold, is it down in the canyon?'

'Lots of gold. Big vein. Old man found it when he was hiding out. Gold in side canyon. On Odom's land. He hates Odom. Odom shot him. Crippled him. Kill Odom and take . . . ' Struggling to breathe, Kale let his words dribble away into silence.

'But why all the night raiding and stealing kids?' Rogue asked, knowing the answer but needing to hear it from someone else.

'He's crazy.'

Rogue nodded and started to get up. Kale gasped in a little breath. 'Rogue,' he said, 'I reckon I'm scared.' He reached out, pawed at Rogue's arm. Rogue took the cold hand and gripped it tight. 'I'm sorry to see you go,' he said, and it was nothing more than the truth. 'You did a brave thing coming here and . . . '

'Not brave. I owed . . . ' He expelled a breath and didn't draw in another.

Rogue stood up, pulled the sheet up to cover the man's face, and said, 'Goodbye Kale. I hope Slim's there, wherever you're going, waiting to ride new trails with you.'

Robby said, his young voice oddly mature, 'I don't think Mama would mind if we buried a man like that in her graveyard.'

'I'm a-thinking there a mort of truth in that,' Shorty said. He struck a sulfur match, took off the smoked-glass chimney, and lit the lamp. After replacing the globe and adjusting the wick to his satisfaction, Shorty reloaded his revolver with fingers that were none too steady. 'Rogue,' he said, clearing his throat twice before he could get the rest of the words out of his mouth. 'I gotta go out to the barn. There was horses and . . . Maybe they didn't all die in the blast and . . . I cain't rightly let no dumb critter suffer.' He cleared his throat as if he intended saying something more, gave his head a quick shake, and walked through the door beside the fireplace.

Robby said, 'I guess I'd better go see if . . . There's probably something that needs doing.' He followed Shorty, but only after he gave Rogue a quick smile, one that was way too full of trust and caring.

Rogue sighed, walked from window to window, pausing at each one to listen intently. He heard nothing except the soft, muffled splash of falling rain. It tempted him, tormented him with visions of pure, unsullied air. The room was stuffy, rank with the smell of black powder, sweat, blood, and death, and it seemed to be closing in around him, making him a prisoner. Knowing it wasn't the wisest thing he had ever done, Rogue unbarred the door, opened it, and stepped out into the refreshing coolness of the night.

The porch floor was wet, rough beneath his stockinged feet, but he felt no discomfort. He sighed again and let his troubling thoughts have full rein of his mind. No matter that he was Lejube Rogue, the demon who walked alone, Faith and her brother had walked into his heart like they owned it. *And maybe they did*.

Holding back another sigh, he let the damp blackness wash around him. He knew he needed time to sort out what had happened to him, time to plan, to think, but there was no more time. The outlaws would be back in the morning, and they would bring dynamite and death for anyone who stood in their way. Kale had given his life to save Faith, and Rogue couldn't let that life be wasted. Could he?

He rested his aching head against one of the peeled poles that held up the porch roof, set his worries free, and waited. For this small time, he would do nothing, except follow the ways Eagle Flying had taught him, let the power build within him, and wait for what would be.

Later — Rogue couldn't have said how much later — Shorty came out onto the porch and said, his voice hoarse with weariness, 'There was four horses killed in the blast. It was a right sorry sight to see and . . . ' His voice trailed off, and he came over to stand in silence beside Rogue.

Finally, Shorty cleared his throat, coughed, and said, 'I reckon it's time we had a talk.'

'Here?' Rogue asked.

'Iffen that's what you want. It don't rightly matter none iffen we go back inside. We laid Kale out in the smokehouse. Haskins is a-snoring away in the kitchen. The boss is with the missus. Robby's standing watch up in the tower and . . . Boy, I don't like to admit it, but I'm plumb tuckered and . . . '

'Let's go in.'

Swallowing hard, quelling the urge to vomit, Rogue followed Shorty back into the stench that filled the room — but maybe what was making him sick wasn't the smell, maybe it was what he was almost afraid to hear: the true story of a murder and a boy, both existing in a long ago time. His voice was almost steady when he said, 'You take the bed. I want to sit up for a while.'

After a nod, Shorty sort of hesitated before he sighed, pulled off his boots, and settled himself on top of the bed.

Rogue waited for him to begin, but it seemed a very long time before Shorty said, 'It hurts some, remembering. I dunno, maybe I ain't doing the right thing, but you have to know. I'll just tell it the way it happened and let you do the deciding about the right or wrong of it. All I ask is that you don't tell the boss.'

'I can promise that.' Rogue eased down on the chair beside the bed, but he didn't relax. He couldn't, and he wasn't sure why.

'Rogue,' Shorty said, speaking so softly that Rogue had to lean closer to hear, 'James Buskirk Odom was a rich, proud, selfish, and right powerful man. He didn't have but one son, the boss, and he brought that boy up to walk in his footsteps. Master Dolph had everything he wanted. He was near spoiled to complete ruination. I reckon it's a mite hard for you know what I'm saying, seeing as how you never had nothing, but even when he was young, his ever word was law. Master Dolph could-a killed me, iffen that had been his notion, and ain't nobody would-a said a word.'

He stopped talking, swallowed, cleared his throat, and then heaved a sigh. 'This part ain't easy, Rogue, but it's gotta be told so's you can know how it was back then.

'Missus Deidre's pa was about the best horse trainer that ever walked the face of the earth. James Buskirk Odom hired him to train his racing stock. He came to the homeplace from Ireland, a-bringing his whole family with him.

'That meant the missus, too, even if she were a married lady with a little boy. Her husband was a rotter, mean to the bone, and he left her with her pa and ma whilst he was out chasing and drinking and acting like he was a-looking for work.

'Master Dolph took him a right powerful hankering for Missus Deidre, but she wouldn't have nothing to do with him.

'But it purely seemed like the more she turned away, the more he wanted her. I reckon he tried everything to tempt her, but she was true to her vows. She smiled a lot and was nice and all, but she managed to stay where there was other folks around. Everbody around knew he was love-struck. Nobody had nerve enough to tell his pa — but they watched, and they sure did a powerful lot of snickering and whispering. A-course they all knew that nothing was a-going to come of it

— 'cepting maybe a sight of heartache. The likes of Missus Deidre, even if she wasn't a married lady, weren't for James Buskirk Odom's son — the Odoms didn't mingle with trash.'

Rogue heard the bitterness and hate in Shorty's voice, but he didn't even wonder at his own curious lack of feelings. Or the beginnings of pity that were melting the ice that encased his soul, pity for the woman who had given him life before she deserted him, ran away with the man who had murdered his father.

Almost as if he could read Rogue's thoughts, Shorty said, 'Don't judge, Rogue, until you know the full truth of it. Until you know what happened when that husband of hers came back and took a job from James Buskirk Odom.'

It was almost totally dark in the room, but Rogue knew Shorty was looking at him, waiting for his answer, so he said, 'Tell me.'

'He moved in with the missus, and it wasn't no time afore she got kinda pale and sick-looking. And she didn't have any smiles in her now — naw, all she had was them bruises where her husband hit her and eyes that spent more time crying than a-sparkling.

'Master Dolph got pale right along with her. He just plain loved her and couldn't rightly stand what was a-happening to her. His pa thought he was sickening, or else he had him an inkling of what was going on, and he sent Master Dolph away — and sent his slave right along with him.

'We traveled around right smart, but Master Dolph couldn't light and set, so about six months or so later we went back home.

'Rogue, when we got there, the first person we saw was Missus Deidre, and she was big with that man's child. Master Dolph he just sort of wilted and died, moped around like his world had plumb ended — and maybe it had; he loved her more'n a man can tell it.

'And there wasn't nothing more between them until Old James gave his party, like he did ever year, for all the trash that worked for him. I reckon he wanted to show everbody how great he was and how nothing they was. I was there that night, a-passing around that fancy food and a-watching them poor folk drink down that liquor and make fools of themselves fawning and scraping to that old bastard.'

The bed creaked as he shifted his weight, but Shorty only paused long enough to take a deep breath, mutter something about this being the hurty part, and go on with the tale. 'Master Dolph was there — his pa had ordered him to come and flatter the poor women with a dance. Well, sir, he danced with ever single one of 'um before he got to Missus Deidre.

'When he went over and ast her, she just shook her head and looked down at the floor. That husband of hers was right there beside her, and he weren't real sober. Now, I don't know why he did it, but he reached out, grabbed that poor woman, and jerked her to her feet.

She kinda swayed, like she were a-feeling faint and was going to fall down right then and there. Master Dolph caught her by the arm and held her up.

'It was purely the wrong thing to do. That husband of hers reared back and screamed, 'That's right, sonny boy, take the slut again. The way I hear it, you been to that well before. That's right, ain't it, Odom? You been lifting her skirt right regular, ain't you?'

'Missus Deidre turned even paler. She moaned, kinda low, and twisted her hands together, but before she could say anything, that husband of hers snatched her away from Master Dolph. Then he screamed something, drew back, and hit her one. It glanced off her jaw. His mad and the whiskey was still riding him so he liked to buried his fist in her stomach, yelling, 'It's in my oven, but it ain't mine, is it, slut?'

'She just sorta crumpled, fell to the floor, hitting her head on a chair on the way down, but her eyes was open, and she was scared.

'Master Dolph was more'n scared, he was mad clean through. He hauled back and hit the man good and solid, knocking him to floor beside Missus Deidre. Cursing, he reached inside his coat and pulled out a little gun, pointed it at Master Dolph, and curled his finger around the trigger.

'Missus Deidre was a-screaming and a-moaning like she was out of her mind. She grabbed that gun and fought with her husband and right in the middle of the ruckus that gun went off. The bullet caught him in the chest. Blood poured out over the both of them, and he was dead in less'n a minute.'

Rogue asked, 'What are you saying? Did my mother kill my father?'

'They was a-fighting and the gun just . . . Son, I don't know. Maybe he shot his own self. I know he was your pa and all, but he was one rotten son-of-a-bitch.'

He had no memory of his father, but if the man took after his father, Enos Scanlon, Rogue's grandfather, then the assessment was probably true, but it didn't make for easy hearing. The silence stretched long before Rogue asked, 'What happened then?'

'All hell broke loose, and hell ain't pretty.'

19

Shorty cleared his throat, said nothing more for a long moment, and then, his voice hoarse with old pain, he said, 'Rogue, it were hell, pure and simple, and I hate to . . . But, I reckon it's gotta be.'

He sighed before he went on with, 'James Buskirk Odom was a-nuther bastard, meaner than any snake, even meaner in his way than your pa, I reckon, but different.

'Old James, he looked down at Missus Deidre and her dead husband a-lying there in a pool of blood, and he kinda turned up his nose and said, 'Get those lazy slaves in here and have these . . . ah . . . people removed. This carpet came from Persia, and it cost a fortune. I will not have it ruined by a pair of . . . Get them out of here at once!'

'Master Dolph gave his pa a real

funny look before he said, 'Deidre saved my life. She needs a . . . '

'The old man lifted that pointy nose even higher and said, 'She needs no reward for doing her duty. You are, after all, my son, and, as such, are far more important than . . . Now, get them out of here, and have the slaves clean this . . . '

'Master Dolph knelt down beside Missus Deidre and took her in his arms. He was a-holding her close against his heart, and his face was twisted something fierce. But he sounded like a real man when he stood up, looked square at that pa of his'n and said, 'If she goes, I go with her. I love her.'

' 'If you have a taste for trash, go, but remember, if you leave with that woman, you are no longer my son.'

'The boss didn't say a word, he just walked out with Missus Deidre in his arms. I followed right along behind. First, we carried her to her own pa's house, but he wouldn't let us in. There was tears running down his face, but he stood real firm when he said, 'She has brought shame to me and mine. I cast her forth and curse her for what she is, a loose woman and a murderess.' He went back inside and closed the door.'

Shorty shifted on the bed, cleared his throat, and refused a drink of water when Rogue offered to get it for him. Silence, broken only by the sighing of the wind, the drip of rain, and house sounds, held them for a long time.

Rogue wasn't sure how he felt about what Shorty was telling him. Relief, maybe, at knowing his mother had done the actual killing, releasing him from his promise to kill the man who had murdered his father. But, what he really felt was nothing, except pity for Shorty and the pain the memories where causing him. The power was strong within him, and it protected him for the moment. He had not a single doubt that Shorty was telling the truth — a truth that left several questions unanswered, questions he wasn't ready to ask.

Shorty took up the tale again. 'Missus Deidre was in real bad shape, and the boss wasn't much better. He was near crazy, but that didn't stop him from doing what needed doing. I held the missus while he stole one of his pa's buggies and a team. We headed for town and the doctor, but we was too late. Missus Deidre lost the baby, and even with that doctor a-fussing and a-dosing, we almost lost her.

'Right about then, the boss went plumb crazy. He was a-ranting and a-raving and a-cussing 'til I was right scared. He kinda claimed her, said she was his'n now and wasn't nobody ever gonna hurt her again, nor bad-mouth her neither. He rousted out a preacher and married the missus right then and right there, not a-knowing if she was a gonna live or die. He set me free at the same time. Sat down beside her bed and wrote out the paper, made that preacher and the doctor sign it, too. He said he reckoned that me nor nobody else was going to go back to his pa.'

Shorty was telling of things long past, but the pain in his voice was as real as if it had all happened the day before. Feeling stifled, smothered by the growing feeling that something was going to happen soon, Rogue stood up. He walked to the fireplace and stood there, leaning against the mantle, waiting to hear the rest of the story — the part that concerned him more directly.

'Rogue,' Shorty said, 'I reckon the rest of it is what you're a-needing to hear, but it sure don't make for good listening. You sure you want me to . . . '

'Yes.' The answer came readily enough, but Rogue couldn't have sworn to the truth of it. The power was still within him, still holding the world at bay, and letting him feel very little. He could only listen — and wait for what would be.

'Old Enos Scanlon, your grandpa, was in town that night. He heard about the ruckus out at Odom's and, being lickered up and not real smart, he came a-looking for the boss, carrying a shotgun he was aiming to use. The boss knocked him down and threw him out of the doc's house, then he followed him out, took the gun, and beat the stock to splinters on the corner of the building.

'That didn't set too well with old Enos. He said, real mean and low, 'I'm a-gonna get you, Odom. I'll follow you to the ends of the earth and on into hell. I'll get you, one way or another, for killing my son.'

'Enos was drunk, like always, and the boss didn't even try to tell him the truth of it. He just said, 'He deserved to die,' and walked back to Missus Deidre.'

Silence rushed in, took full possession of the room. It lasted an eternity or longer before Rogue asked, 'What of Deidre's son? Didn't anyone care about him?'

Shorty cleared his throat, cleared it again. His voice almost inaudible, he said, 'I'm real sorry, Rogue, but I reckon nobody even thought about the boy. Missus Deidre wasn't in no shape to be a-thinking about anything. The boss? Well, right about then, he was a troubled man who was a-caring about one thing, and that was the missus. And me, all I was a-caring about was the boss. And even later, that was the way of it.

'We did us a fair amount of moving around and . . . Well, it shames me to say it, but when we heard that old Enos had taken the boy, the boss figgered the kid wouldn't amount to much. Along about then, he told Missus Deidre the boy was dead. Cholera, I reckon.'

Rogue had heard all he needed to know, but Shorty wasn't through with his talking. 'She took the news real good, didn't cry much or do any carrying-on right then. It weren't till we came west, in '57, that she took bad. And that wasn't till after her other babies came and died. But, you don't want to hear about that, 'cause it's over, ain't it?'

There was no real answer Rogue could give. 'Is it?' he asked, hoping it was, but knowing it wasn't.

'It has to be. We knew that old devil was a-following us, a-looking to kill the boss and maybe Missus Deidre, too. And we knew he were a-dragging the little boy everywhere he went, but the boss didn't want the boy found and brought here — not with the way the missus was about then.

'We was right glad when we heard old Enos and Patrick was both dead out in the Nevada desert somewheres. It relieved the boss' mind a mite and . . . ' Shorty sighed heavily and then said, 'I knew who you was when we found you out in the rocks. I'm a-thinking the boss knew you, too, but he didn't hold your past agin you. He did the right thing, didn't he? He . . . ' Shorty stopped, cleared his throat, and asked, 'When I was a-doctoring you, I couldn't help seeing . . . Did old Enos put them scars on your back?'

'Yes.'

'I'm sorry. I reckon I knew what kinda devil he was, but I . . . '

'Did Odom know?'

'Rogue, I reckon he did, but you gotta try to understand. That boy wasn't a blamed thing to the boss. All he cared about was . . . Dag nab it, I knew I should-a kept my fool mouth shut. Now, I . . . Rogue, will you leave now, leave peaceable and not . . . '

'Shorty, some things are mine to do, and I can't leave until they are done.'

'Please don't . . . '

'It's almost morning, you'd better get some sleep.'

'I've been square with you, Rogue, but I . . . I reckon I got the right to say it. There's a sight of tales going around about Lejube Rogue and the things he can do, magical things some folks say. Now, I know you ain't no demon, but couldn't you just . . . well, sort of fix everthing and . . . '

'No.'

Shorty made a grumbling sound

deep in his throat, but he didn't say another word.

Rogue stretched, tested the strength returning to his healing body. He was still stiff and sore, but the power was with him, giving him more than enough strength to do what he needed to do. Walking softly, his stockinged feet making little whispers of sound on the puncheon floor, he walked out to meet the coming day. The storm had passed. Gray light filled the sky. Taking in deep breaths of the rain-washed air, he waited for the household to wake, waited until he could get his carbine and his moccasins. He would fulfill his promise to Faith this day.

The sun was still below the eastern horizon, but the silvery pink of dawn was spreading across the sky when Odom walked out onto the porch and came to where Rogue stood at the railing. He asked, 'Did that outlaw say anything more before he died?'

'They're coming back today or

tonight to dynamite the house.'

'Well, you go get some rest. I'll call you if I need you, but there's really nothing you can do now.'

'As soon as I get some of my gear, I'm going after them.'

'No. You're not going anywhere.'

Still keeping his voice low, Rogue said, 'I'm going.'

'Well,' Odom said, looking off into the distance, 'I don't suppose a little scouting would hurt. I'll have Haskins round up some horses and we . . . '

'No horses.'

'Don't act like a fool, you need . . . '

'I am going now. I'm going on foot, and I'm going alone.'

Odom turned to glare at Rogue. 'No,' he said, like he was giving orders to one of his children, 'you're going to stay here where you belong.'

'I don't belong here. Whatever claim you might have had on me, you gave up long ago. Now, get my moccasins and my Spencer.'

'But, I . . . '

'Don't worry, Odom. They won't kill me.'

'So, what you're telling me is that you'll be back.'

Rogue tried to explain, to tell the man he had made a promise to Faith. When it was over, he had to come back to tell her she was safe. He said, 'Odom, I made a promise . . . '

Odom interrupted, 'I'm fully aware of that. I know you'll be back, and then we'll meet. I'll be waiting for you, and you'd better remember that I'm no drunken outlaw. And, just so you know, when I shoot, I shoot to kill.' He turned and stomped away before Rogue could say another word.

Rogue shook his head. He had tried to tell the rancher that the promise Patrick Scanlon had made to his dying grandfather wouldn't be kept. Well, he thought, there'll be time to do it later, after he had taken care of the outlaws. And, if the outlaws took care of him, the whole problem was solved. He was still standing there, looking toward the door to the house when Faith slipped out, his battered footgear clutched against her chest.

'Here,' she whispered, 'take them quick. Daisy's on a tear, and she burned the rest of your stuff. Robby had these, and she didn't know where they were.'

'Thanks.' He leaned over and pulled on the fringed moccasins, giving her a smile when he found the knife still safely in its sheath. His smile was gone when he straightened. He looked down at her, and said, as gently as he could, 'Faith, I'm going after them. I have to, you know that, don't you?'

She nodded. 'Do you have to go right now?'

'Yes.'

'But . . . ' She stopped. Her chin and lower lip stared to quiver, and there was a shine of wetness in her eyes.

'Tears?' Rogue asked, trying to keep his voice light, to hide the ache that was starting in his own throat.

'You're my brother and I . . . I won't cry, honest.'

'Never again?'

'I promise. I won't cry for you, but I will love . . . I will always love . . . ' she hesitated, licked her lips, and then whispered the last word, 'you.'

The lump in Rogue's throat almost choked him. Almost against his will, his hand reached out to brush back the little girl's tangled hair, but he couldn't allow himself to finish the loving gesture.

His hand was at his side, but love was in his eyes and his heart when he stood and watched as she ran back into the house. 'They won't touch you, Faith. I swear it,' he said, and maybe he said the words aloud.

20

Rogue limped across the yard, stepping around muddy puddles and the sprawled bodies of dead outlaws. He wanted to feel something, but even though he had killed them, Rogue felt no guilt. They had tried to harm two innocent children; and, according to the way Rogue felt about that, the men deserved what they got.

A hundred yards or so west of the log house, Rogue entered a small grove of aspen. The leaves fluttered and quaked, silver and green, dancing with a breeze so slight that nothing else moved from its breath. This was his world, and he knew it well. But other men had been here before him, and they had left a trail of ugliness to mark their passage.

Horses had stamped and turned within the grove, leaving hoofprint that had been softened by the heavy rain.

Bullets had ripped through trees and saplings and tore weeping gashes in their white bark. Grass and brush were crushed and broken. Empty brass cartridges littered the torn earth.

Following the outlaws' spoor, Rogue left the trees, moving west away from the huddle of ranch buildings across a broad, upward sloping meadow. He didn't look back, but when he reached the tree line, he heard someone calling his name.

Rogue stopped, turned, waited for the boy who was running in his direction. Robby held a rifle in one hand, and a bulging sack in the other. He wore a gunbelt strapped around his skinny hips and the holstered .45 banged against his thigh with every step he took. He stopped when he was close. Chest heaving, he gasped for enough breath to say, 'I'm going with you.'

For an instant, Rogue didn't know what to say, didn't know whether to order the boy back or . . . Finally, he asked, 'Why?' and it was a sincere need for knowing.

Robby scuffed the rain-soaked ground with the toe of his boot and swallowed hard. He raised his head, looked Rogue square in the face, and said, 'Faith is my little sister, too.'

The boy's quiet words hurt, hurt deep, and it wasn't a hurt that Rogue welcomed. He took a quick breath, but could find no words to either deny the boy or accept him as a brother.

Gripping the rifle with white knuckled hands, Robby moved uneasily, but there was no uncertainty in his voice when he said, 'She's really scared and . . . Rogue, I don't want her to be sick like Mama.'

'What about your father, does he know . . . '

'I didn't sneak off,' Robby said, lifting his chin a little higher before he added, 'I told him I was going with you.'

'And?'

'He didn't say much, he just looked

at me real funny and turned his back, like he was ashamed or something, and then he told me to go ahead if that's what I had to do.' After a moment the boy said, his voice barely above a whisper, 'Faith told me you are our brother. Patrick. The one that's supposed to be dead.'

After a brief nod of acknowledgment, Rogue stood there trying to sort out the emotions that were trying to crowd into his head — emotions held at bay by the power. 'What's in the sack?' he asked, an innocent question to ease the tension between them.

'Some boiled ham and cold biscuits. Daisy's on a tear, so Faith helped me steal them.'

'Sounds good to me. Now all we need is a little water to wash them down with.'

A grin spread across Robby's face. 'Do — do you want me to show you?'

'You bet. I hope you stole a bunch because I haven't had any breakfast.'

'Neither have I,' Robby said with

another grin as he led his brother on up the hillside into the forest. They climbed quietly, moving up the needle-slick slope slowly and cautiously. The steep ridge was a large one. Moving at an angle that paralleled the trail left by the outlaws, they circled rocky bluffs, crawled over fallen logs, and fought their way through brush. At the top, they paused for a moment's rest.

The view to the north gave Rogue a twinge of unease. Thunderheads towered, black and threatening, and they were very obviously speeding south, heading toward Rogue and Robby. Knowing he could do nothing to quell the force of the storm, Rogue shook his head.

Robby said, 'The spring's about a hundred yards down and to the left, if you still want to eat.'

Rogue nodded and followed where the boy led. The spring was a disappointment to them both. In other seasons, when the earth wasn't storm-soaked, the water was probably only a trickle, dripping down stained rocks into a moss-lined basin, but now it poured and rushed muddily down the hillside.

Looking at the spate, Robby flushed. 'I'm sorry. I've never been here when . . . I guess Pa's right. I guess I really can't do anything right.'

'You're not in charge of storms, Robby,' Rogue said, keeping his voice soft. 'It doesn't matter. It's a good place to stop and do a little planning.' It was a sheltered cove, almost surrounded by firs and big boulders — a place of shelter from discovery should any of the outlaws be standing guard.

Leaning his rifle against a tree trunk, Robby pulled thick slabs of ham and large sourdough biscuits from the bag. They ate standing and Rogue walked around to keep his leg limber. They were both silent until Robby said, 'I've been thinking about what Kale said. You know, there at the end, just before he died?'

Rogue took another bite, nodded,

311

and waited for the boy to continue.

Thunder growled in the distance, and Robby said, 'I think I know where the outlaw camp is. Pa's got a lot of land up here, and it's mostly all mountains and canyons. But in this direction, there's only one canyon that goes into South Fork Canyon. I even know where the cave is because there's only one that's actually a cave. And it's not much.'

'Where from here?' Rogue asked.

'Just over the next ridge is where the canyon starts.

'It's pretty steep at the upper end. It drains a lot of snow melt and, well, sometime or another, a big flood dug out all the dirt from under part of the east wall in a spot about thirty feet long and maybe ten or twelve feet deep. And it's high enough for a horse to stand under real easy. The cave itself is right in the middle of the undercut and it goes back into the cliff eight or nine feet and then makes a sharp turn to the right. I don't know how far it goes from there because Pa wouldn't let me go any further. He said the whole thing would probably come crashing down.'

Robby licked his lips. 'It has to be the place.

'There's drinking water, wood left by floods and stuff, and a cattle trail down to the water about a quarter of a mile up from the cave. They could take their horses down it easy.'

Thunder rumbled again, louder. The sky was growing darker. Clouds were scudding in their direction.

'It sounds right to me,' Rogue said, finishing the last of his ham. 'It'll be rain soon, so we'd better get moving.' After a quick look at the boy, he asked, 'Are you scared?'

'Yes, but I'm going anyway.'

Almost against his will, Rogue reached out, put his hand on Robby's shoulder. 'Robby,' he said, meaning every word, 'I'm proud to know you. It takes a brave man to admit his fear and keep on going.'

'Rogue, I . . . ' Robby ducked his head, grinned a little, and then asked,

'When this is over, will you stay?'

'I can't. I guess we both know that. Besides, it's best if your mother continues to believe her Patrick is dead.'

'But . . . '

'No, Robby?'

'You can't just ride away and forget us. You belong to us now.'

'No.'

'You'll break Faith's heart. She loves you.'

'She knows I can't stay.'

'But . . . '

'We can hash this out later. Let's get out of here.'

Suiting action to his words, Rogue left the hidden spring with Robby close behind, just as the first few sprinkles of rain came down from the building storm.

A lot less than an hour later, plodding through the pouring rain, they moved together down the far side of the second mountain ridge. Fully aware they must be getting close, Rogue whispered, 'How far?'

'The cave is less than a half a mile away. The head of the canyon is right there.' Robby pointed, and Rogue could see the eroded, red clay walls of a gully just beyond where they stood. He set their plan of action.

'Robby,' he said, 'we're going to have to split up. I want you to follow the canyon down, but stay on top of the west wall. Can you do that?'

'Yes. What are you going to do?'

'I'm going in.'

'But . . .'

'Robby, keep even with me, but stay low. Don't let them see you. Watch for guards.'

'Okay.'

'Robby,' Rogue said slowly, 'it's not going to be easy or pretty, but . . .'

'I know,' the boy answered, but it seemed as if it was a man who spoke, a man who would do what had to be done. It made Rogue ache, but all he did was hold out his hand. His brother shook it. And nothing more was said, not even farewell, as they slid down the slick walls of the gully together, Rogue boosted Robby up the other side, and they parted. Rogue caught brief glimpses of the boy as they traveled downward, toward the outlaws, but only when Robby deliberately showed himself. Rogue smiled, and it held real fondness, but it was fleeting, giving way to the death chant that crowded his throat, came soft out of his mouth.

It was, as Eagle Flying had taught him, a good day to die. And the power was strong within him. Rogue was ready.

The canyon walls grew taller, steeper, changed from clay to granite. The floor widened. Springs seeped from cracks in the cliffs, ran down, formed a brook. The tiny stream grew larger and larger as more runoff joined its course. Muddied and swollen by the storm, it grew into a torrent that grumbled and roared as it raced down the rock-filled canyon.

Limping heavily, slipping and sliding, his injured legs trembling under his weight, Rogue went on, determined. The footing was treacherous. Rocks rolled beneath his feet. One patch of slick clay sent him to his knees. But he refused to let his battered body surrender. Wiping his muddy hands on his shirt, he pulled himself erect. Using the rocky wall as support, he went on.

The canyon narrowed. The muddy water splashed and boiled through the channel, beat against the bases of both walls. The rain still pounded down, and he was already dripping wet — more water wasn't going to hurt him. But it wasn't going to help him either.

Rogue studied the passage, took a deep breath, and waded into the icy water. Edging along the face of the eastern cliff, he fought the pull of the furious water. The next step caught him off-balance, plunged him into a deep hole, and threw him, full-length, into the flood.

Sputtering and shivering, he managed to reach the wall, pull himself up. He stood, gripped the rocks, and breathed heavily. The fall had added new pain to what already throbbed in his thigh, and now his chest burned with every breath he took. Despite his pain, he moved on — only a trifle slower.

The canyon narrowed more and curved sharply to the right, hiding what lay ahead. The swift water swirled around Rogue's waist by the time he reached the curve. Cautiously, he peeked around the stone barrier.

The stone walls were no more than eight feet apart, and there was another bend in the canyon some thirty feet from where he stood. The towering walls leaned inward, almost touching at the top, shutting out what little daylight there was. The real barrier was the raging, foaming, leaping cauldron of water.

He paused, tried to think, to come up with some useable plan. The heavy, almost deafening roar of the flood beat against him. He couldn't go back or try to find some way around — there wasn't time — but he couldn't go on. There were no ledges or handholds on the walls, and he hadn't enough strength to swim it.

Taking a small step forward, Rogue tried to find some way through the turbulent trap. A mossy rock rolled beneath his moccasins. He floundered, waved his arms, tried to regain his balance. Failed. Fell. Feet first he went, into the surging torrent.

Tumbling and rolling in the current, he fought, tried to stay afloat. Slammed into a rock. Grabbed at it. Slid away. Went under. Came up. Went under. And was swept around the bend and thrown into a broad, shallow pool. Coughing and choking, Rogue crawled to the eastern shore and sprawled, nearly unconscious, on the rain-soaked rocks.

He lay without moving, fighting to regain his breath. Finally, he mustered enough strength to turn his head, saw a flicker of motion, a dark shadow, stared at it, tried to focus.

What finally swam into view wasn't much to his liking. A dirty, unshaven man stood over him, grinning wolfishly. The muzzle of the gun he held was pointed at Rogue's head, and the man's trigger finger was curled and ready.

21

Dazed, his mind not quite tracking, Rogue stared at the gun muzzle for a second before he shifted his gaze to the man. He was one of the outlaws, he had to be, but at the moment, that bit of information didn't seem to be of any great importance.

'Well,' the man said, his voice harsh, gloating, and holding a full sneer, 'I never figgered nobody'd be stupid enough to come through that death trap, but I ain't real sorry you did. The old man won't be neither. Get up, and let's go pay him a little visit.'

The power fairly raging through him, holding all else at a distance, Rogue saw no reason to either move or speak. He just lay there, gathering his strength, waiting for what would happen.

'I'm a-thinking you're that there Rogue. The old man's nephew has been a-ranting and a-swearing about you ever since he pulled in here. According to Mister Ben, you're one hell of a tough son, but you don't rightly look all that tough to me.'

Pretending to be weaker than he actually felt, Rogue groaned.

'What's the matter? Ain't scared, are you? Hell, considering Mister Ben and that yellow-livered bunch-a blowhards, maybe I'm the first real man you ever had to face. That's right, ain't it?' His laugh was as unpleasant as his voice.

Rogue groaned again.

'Get up!'

Letting his body go completely limp, Rogue didn't move.

The outlaw holstered his .44 and reached back, pulled a Bowie knife from a sheath on his belt. 'Playing possum ain't gonna get you out of this, 'cause I got me a notion to do me a little carving on that mug of yourn. Or maybe I just ought-a whack out that tongue of yourn.'

He leaned closer. 'Yeah, that's it. The

old man promised me I could use my knife on that little girl, but you sneaked and grabbed her. I reckon you owe me for that.'

Rogue tensed. He had to take the man out, and soon, and do it as quietly as possible. The rest of the gang had to be somewhere near. But how was he going to do it? He still didn't have a plan when the man reached down, grabbed him by the shoulder, and flopped him over on his back. The man was grinning and his knife was ready. It came closer.

A blur of motion on top the far wall caught Rogue's attention. The fist-sized rock that slammed down into the outlaw's back was all that man knew before he grunted with pain and slashed down with the knife, barely notching Rogue's ear. That galvanized him into immediate action.

Rogue's left knee came up, drove into the man's groin. Writhing but still ready to use the knife, the man fell across Rogue's chest. Rogue grabbed his wrist, held the knife away from his own throat. They struggled silently. Rocked back and forth. Rolled off the rocks. Splashed into the muddy water. Fought, punched, tore, gouged.

The outlaw kicked Rogue's injured thigh. Rogue convulsed with the pain, shoved hard against the man's knife hand. The outlaw made a gurgle of sound as the sharp blade slashed his throat. His blood was lost in the flood of muddy water. Rogue held the lifeless body for a moment before he dropped it, struggled to his feet, and staggered back to the shore.

Once there, he looked up. Robby loomed black against the grayness of the sky. The boy waved, dropped the rock he held, and waited. Rogue returned the wave, added a brief salute, and pointed down the canyon.

Robby pointed the same way and disappeared from Rogue's sight, leaving Rogue to limp and stumble on down the rock-filled canyon alone.

The high walls cut off much of the

icy rain, but it didn't matter. Rogue didn't feel the chill, the blood dripping down from his ear; he didn't feel anything. His leg was numb. His physical strength was almost gone, but the power raged within him, forced him on.

A large boulder jutted out from the wall, reaching almost to the water's edge. Rogue checked his Colts before he eased around the tower of stone. Moving cautiously, he limped along its base, peered around the curving edge.

A man was there, standing guard. Hat pulled low to ward off the rain, huddled in a yellow slicker, the man was sitting close to the stone, his back turned to Rogue. A muddy trail angled up and was lost in the rocks of the canyon wall. The outlaws' horses were loosely corralled at the foot of the trail, just beyond the man.

Rogue pulled one six-shooter, gripped it by the barrel, raised it shoulder high, and slipped around the boulder. A rock rolled beneath his water-soaked moccasins, made a slight clatter of sound. The guard's head lifted, started to turn. Rogue's Colt thudded down, contacted. The man pitched forward, unconscious.

Rogue tugged at the limp body until it was out of sight, hidden behind some brush. Only then did he look down and recognize Ben. He wanted to shoot him, but he couldn't, not when the man was defenseless.

The horses moved restlessly, backed away from Rogue and the ropes that formed their corral. Pulling the knife from his moccasin, Rogue cut through the ropes, setting them free. With very little encouragement from him, they started up the trail and out of the canyon.

The outlaw camp had to be near. Rogue went on. Slower. Slipping from rock to rock, glancing at the top of the opposite wall, hoping the boy was keeping himself safe. Robby was nowhere to be seen. Rogue rounded another curve and saw the outlaws.

They were close — too damned close.

Breath caught in his throat, and he stopped. A glass bottle arched through the rain, crashed into the rocks in front of him. Slowly, deadly, the power a torrent ready to be unleashed, Rogue moved on, moved toward the outlaws sheltering under the rocky overhang that was exactly as Robby had described it.

Closer. Closer still. The power owned him, put death in his eyes, in his hands. Totally unaware he had drawn them, the Colts were cocked and ready. His forefingers curled around the triggers. His death chant rose in his throat and left his mouth to echo over and over in the confines of the canyon.

'Butler, he's coming!' The shout came from above and to Rogue's right. He turned and fired. A guard toppled from a rocky perch, and the lead from his six-gun crashed into the earth at Rogue's feet.

Outlaws scurried, cursed, ran. Gun-fire boomed. Rogue went on, shooting as he moved forward. Lead whined and splatted around him. Chipping rocks. Tearing the earth. Ricocheting wildly.

The chant grew louder; Rogue walked on. He had seen the pile of wooden boxes, read the bold black letters, knew the dynamite was stacked close against the back wall of the shallow cave. It and a box of blasting caps.

Rogue's lip drew back into a smile, a wolfish smile. He still had one cartridge in either gun. That would be enough. Standing tall, he aimed, shot. The hot lead slammed into the smaller box. Rogue wasn't disappointed.

Sound exploded, blasted, tore. Rock groaned and lifted. Men screamed. The earth buckled, moved. Boulders, flew, crashed, smashed. The great cliff ripped, thundered, fell, and fell, and fell. Men died.

Fury roared through the canyon, threw Rogue up and back, silenced his chant with dirt and dust and stone. He fell, splashed into the stream. Rocks and dirt hailed down, thudded, rolled, crashed, broke, and, finally, were still.

The thunderous sound died an uneasy death. The rain pelted down on the gigantic rockslide that replaced the cave, blocked the canyon, and buried a gang of outlaws. The stream backed up behind the rocky tomb. Only Rogue lived.

Deafened by the blast, he crawled, mindless, to the east shore and dropped, unconscious. The promise he had made to Faith was kept, the power was gone, nothing drove him now — he could rest.

Later, how much later Rogue didn't know, he heard someone. Felt someone pulling at him, shouting his name.

'Rogue! Please! You have to!'

His tongue didn't want to shape words, but he tried.

'Wha . . . '

Robby, or at least he thought it was Robby, said, 'You're in the water. The blast dammed the canyon. The water is rising fast. You have to move. Come on. Get up.'

'The outlaws?' Rogue mumbled.

'Ben got away. The rest of them are dead and buried.'

Rogue's strength seeped back and brought a dribble of power with it. He knew he wasn't finished. Ben was still alive.

Robby tugged at his arm. 'Rogue, I can't lift you. You have to move.'

'How did you get here?'

Taking a deep breath, Robby pulled at him again. 'I threw the rifle away and climbed down the wall. I thought you were dead and . . . ' His voice wavered, shook itself into silence, but after a moment, the boy went on, 'Are you hurt bad? There's blood all over you.'

'Cuts,' Rogue said, somehow knowing it was the truth but still trying to find a clear path through the muddle that filled his aching head.

'Can you move?' his brother asked, the worry in his voice making it climb high.

'Ben?'

'He went up the trail after the horses. Can you move?'

'Yes,' Rogue said. 'Have to. Have to kill Ben — a mad dog. Won't give up until your whole family is destroyed.' He got to his hands and knees, his face almost touching the water. Faintly dizzy, he shook his head. His ears rang. The bloody water running into his eyes almost blinded him. He reached up, took Robby's hand, and let the boy help him stand. Swaying like a wind-blown tree, he stood a moment, trying to make sense of the chaos all around him, the enormous pile of broken stone that blocked the canyon, the rising water. 'None of them got away?'

'No. I watched. There wasn't even time for them to whimper. When the dynamite went, the whole cliff lifted up in the air and came straight down on top of them before it sort of spilled out into the canyon floor.'

'Faith won't have to worry about them,' Rogue muttered. 'I find Ben, she won't have to worry about him either. Come on, Robby.'

'The ranch is . . . You can't . . . '

'Can. Will.' Rogue fumbled for his Colts. They were both gone.

'Here,' Robby said, handing his own revolver to Rogue. 'It's loaded.'

The brothers walked out of the canyon together, and headed back to the ranch. They moved slowly, rested often, but eventually the canyon and dead outlaws were far behind them. Sometime during their trek, the rain had quit, and in the west a few weak, watery rays of sunlight poked holes in a tattered bank of gray clouds.

Rogue had gathered new strength along the way. Robby cut a staff for him, and he leaned heavily on it. He walked alone, silently, scanning the timber, constantly seeking Ben. He knew Ben had to be near and probably near-mad: his uncle was dead and the gold buried; Ben was a known crook, a man with nothing left to lose; and Ben was a coward, a sneak who would hide so as to shoot a man in the back.

Finally, they could see the big meadow, far down the slope, beyond the screen firs. The ranch was close, but Rogue's unease was chewing at him, growing larger by the moment. Suddenly he caught a flash of blue. Something or someone was climbing the slope not far below them.

He hissed a warning, took shelter behind the trunk of a huge Ponderosa pine. Robby dropped down behind a fallen log. Rogue took careful note of their surroundings.

A small clearing lay directly in front of them. A steep, brush-grown bluff bordered it on the right; the left was open timber. At the foot of the glade, wild plums, lilacs, and huckleberry brush had grown, interwoven to a dense thicket. The flash of blue had been beyond the thicket's lower edge.

Robby's six-shooter in his hand, Rogue waited, tense and ready, watching for the bit of blue, some betraying motion. And his heart did an odd little flop when his prey came into sight. He stared at Faith, dressed in blue gingham, and at the old man that walked beside her, a blind old Man of Power leading two horses: one a roan and one Rogue's dapple stallion, Ghost. Eagle Flying had come. How or why didn't matter. Joy almost too great to be contained raced through Rogue, gave him hope.

Moving in his direction, Faith and Eagle Flying talked quietly, walked straight toward where Rogue stood, but they weren't alone. Carrying a rifle, looking like he fully intended to use it, Dolph Odom walked about twenty feet behind his daughter.

All joy left his body, left only Lejube Rogue, the ice-eyed demon as Ben stood up in the thicket and aimed his pistol at Odom's back.

'Behind you, Odom!' Rogue shouted and fired his gun to save the life of the man he had hunted for years. As his handgun spat fire, Rogue saw Odom lift his rifle and point the muzzle at his heart. He saw the last outlaw die just before he heard Faith scream, 'No, Papa!' and knew Dolph Odom was shooting to kill. Shooting to kill Lejube Rogue.

Rogue saw red blossom on Ben's chest before he dropped his own gun and waited for Dolph Odom to fire.

It wasn't a long wait.

Thus ended the tale of Lejube Rogue, the gun-fighter, the demon without friend or family, who died as he had lived.

★ ★ ★

But there are other tales with other endings, tales that speak of an empty grave in Dolph Odom's burying ground, of a blind old Indian shaman that stopped Odom's bullet, caught it in his left hand before it could do any harm, and said, 'Would you kill him twice? Leave be. All debts are paid. Carve a marker with his name to save his mother from further hurt, lay the demon legend to rest in a coffin that holds no bones. Give him peace.'

* * *

The rainy winter nights were long and dark. The eternal winds sang a mournful song. Many tales were told by the lonely pioneers as the hearthfire fell to ash and ember.

Some were true.

THE END